TAMING KANE

A DARK PARANORMAL ROMANCE

FATED MATES
BOOK 1

TESSA STONE

CONTENT WARNINGS

This story contains material that some readers may find disturbing or objectionable, including:

Violence and gore - The story contains scenes depicting violence between supernatural creatures, including graphic descriptions of injuries and death.

Kidnapping and threats - A main character is kidnapped and threatened.

Sexual content - The story contains explicit sexual content, including non-consensual advances and rough sex.

Supernatural themes - The story centers around supernatural creatures like shifters, vampires, and witches. It contains magical elements and violence related to these themes.

Language - The story uses graphic language and profanity.

Other content - The story explores mature themes like sex trafficking, radicalism, pregnancy, and discrimination. Some scenes feature tense dynamics between characters.

Please carefully consider whether the content is right for you before reading further. While sensitively handled, this material could potentially trigger or disturb some readers. Let's discuss if you have any other concerns! I'm happy to clarify specific details that might help inform your decision. The goal is to help you engage thoughtfully with challenging creative work.

PROLOGUE

Kane

Memories of the Great War 1000 A.D.

Scandinavia

I stand before King Amir's throne with my brother Levi, our newly appointed alpha, as he kneels and admits our failure. We lost the Great War against the humans, largely due to the betrayal of the Bailey Witches.

King Amir summoned us from Kenya to aid in the fight. Those witches, falling for humans they aren't even destined to mate with, defied our Goddess Fate's law. They are our eternal enemies now. King Amir sits motionless, his golden eyes distant.

Born in the Mesopotamian era, of the Bailey witch bloodline, his age is a mystery. He warned us, before retreating to the mountains from Egypt, that a curse would fall upon us if we lost the war. A curse that would doom all supernaturals to purgatory. He planned this war for thousands of years, hoping Fate would favor us. Yet, here we stand, defeated.

"House of Zorah, and all packs, clans, prides, and covens before me, it is with great regret that we have failed to defeat the humans. The curse is upon us, and we must endure," King Amir says in a low tone, his mind seemingly elsewhere.

Levi rises first, and we follow. The rest of the court lifts their heads. King Amir's face is stone-like, a rare sight.

"Forgive me, my Lord, but what does this mean for us?" Levi asks, eyes fixed on the floor, avoiding the king's gaze. The palace is thick with fear and curiosity, but King Amir's scent is different—it's pain, agony.

King Amir stands, and the room falls silent. His brown fingers touch his lips, his sharp, translucent nails brushing over them as he ponders.

"We must endure the shadows. It will feel as if time has stopped. The Bailey Witches' curse will trap us in a timeless purgatory, defying our Goddess Fate's laws. But know this: the curse will run its course. Our destiny to rule this earth as true leaders is set. The prophecy has begun." He removes his crown, causing gasps and whispers to ripple through the enormous room.

"Now, I understand, my youngling, why I've birthed her. I thought this was punishment for turning a witch, a law I've broken by Fate, but now I see it was necessary. You will all go into the shadows, out of humanity's sight until the curse is lifted. I do not know the day or the year, but I do know you will be set free and paired with your fated mates. For now, they are lost to you, as mine is lost to me." With that, King Amir bows his head before us, an act of true submission as a leader, and then he turns away, leaving us to our thoughts.

I won't know what it feels like to have a mate? This is what I was born for, to be paired with a woman destined for me to serve, protect, provide for, and love. I won't get to know what it feels like to have children, small pups of my own? I won't get to enjoy the warmth of her and love her the way my parents did?

I've already lost so much in this war. My parents are dead, the majority of my pack is gone, leaving just me and my brothers. At this moment, I wish I had died in battle. This sentence is far worse than death. I don't want to live on like this. Levi turns to us, and I can see the hurt in his eyes. King Amir doesn't have to stay to explain; we all know the prophecy he's told us for centuries. I'm three hundred years old and I won't age anymore until I'm paired with my fated mate.

I don't understand this curse. Fate, our Goddess, why can't she help us right now? My heart feels like it's going to burst at the thought of not having my woman—my rib, the one who gives my life meaning. She's just been taken from me.

Human men are to blame for this. These blasted witches have taken away my reason for living. I've lost the one thing that made me keep pushing through this existence.

My mate. My hope. My everything.

"House of Zorah," Levi announces, and I immediately stand at attention, tears welling in my eyes, but I don't let them fall. I can see the pain in my brother's eyes, the hurt of losing our parents, the majority of our pack, and now our true happiness—our mates. Yet he finds a way to stand strong. A true Alpha, he will forever have my respect and honor for this.

"We will follow our king's orders. We will endure." With his words, I fall to my knees in submission to him; the word of my Alpha is law. Levi draws in a breath as we separate, tribes no longer one. The packs, prides, clans, and covens all retreat from the throne, disappearing into the purgatory that begins now.

Why is Fate punishing us? What did we do? We've honored her laws, kept to the best of our abilities. Why is she leaving us to rot like this? I rise when my brother, my alpha, raises his hand, standing side by side with Gabriel and Micah, my two other brothers who are also doing their best to hold it together.

"We will survive this, I promise you," Levi assures us, his voice firm and resolute. When Levi takes a step, we move aside, opening a pathway for him to lead the way.

He leads us out of the palace and immediately shifts into his wolf form—a large, black wolf with silver eyes. My brothers and I follow, transforming into our wolves as well. Levi's wolf takes the lead, and we sprint from the palace into the depths of the forest. I know his plan: find a temporary spot to stay until we decide our next move. We're nomads now, with no place to call home.

Without our fated mates, we have no true home. We just exist. As we move deeper into the forest, my wolf stops, drawn to the full moon lighting up the sky. He howls, pleading for Fate's mercy. It's pointless; we can't change this. This is Fate's decision. She hasn't intervened. We have to endure.

So, we will.

1

_____

Tami

Y ou know what I hate most about Christmas?
Holiday lights. I'm standing in the garage of my
client's house, cursing myself for agreeing to this.
Of course, they didn't properly store the lights from last
year. It's going to take my whole shift to detangle this mess
and wrap it around the tree.

I put a finger to my lips, wondering if I could get away
with driving to the dollar store and dropping twenty bucks
on a new set. I would've wasted the money on a pizza
anyway. But then again, this is a wealthy neighborhood;
Sally will notice cheap lights from across the room. I sigh,
grab the box, and head back into the house to start the
detangling process. I glare at Angie, my co-worker on this
shift, realizing why she's been so nice to me this week.

It's because she didn't want to do this, spend a day
unraveling Christmas lights.

She gives me a wicked grin and turns back to the stove to
finish preparing dinner. We're both CNAs, working the

afternoon shift in a shared housing unit for the elderly. We take care of Sally, a seventy-year-old retired teacher with dementia, and Julie, a seventy-five-year-old retired nurse who's wheelchair-bound. They share this house as room-mates but need round-the-clock care.

It's good money taking on gigs like this, and I love Sally and Julie. They bicker like an old married couple but can't live without each other. It's fun to watch. These lovely women carry so much wisdom, giving Angie and me a few pointers in the love department. They've had their glory days, and their stories are fascinating.

Sadly, in situations like this, the elderly tend to be forgotten, and their families rarely come around. They'll stop by for Christmas, where Angie and I have to force smiles, knowing they don't really care about these wonderful women. They're just doing their good deed for the year.

But that's alright. I've adopted Sally and Julie as my family while I'm employed here. I don't have a family of my own. I grew up in the foster care system, moving from house to house. but I know better than to get too attached. The moment I leave this job, I won't be able to see them anymore. I have Tiffany, my roommate and best friend, but she's got her own demons, and our friendship seems to be slowly falling apart.

Without Sally, Julie, and Angie, I'm all alone. And it doesn't help that I'm struggling in the dating department. I can't seem to find anyone, and I'm starting to wonder if I'm the problem.

"Look on the bright side, Tami. You can spend the day daydreaming while untangling those lights," Angie teases. I stick my tongue out and give her the finger in response, scowling when I see my chipped nail. I really need to stop working so hard and take better care of myself. I'm starting to fall apart.

She stirs the pot of spaghetti, the aroma filling the kitchen. Angie's cooking is always top-notch. She dreams of becoming a personal chef, and with her skills, she won't be in this job much longer. After setting the pot to simmer, she washes her hands and turns on the small TV mounted on the wall.

"Damn, if I had the money," she mutters, eyes glued to the screen. Another vacation ad.

"Are you ready for the vacation of a lifetime?" the announcer's voice booms.

Angie grabs a gallon of milk from the fridge, leaning against the counter, her gaze still fixed on the TV. The screen shows stunning winter landscapes, luxurious accommodations, and supernatural beings—all seamlessly integrated into the scenes.

"Welcome to Wintermoon," the announcer continues, "your ultimate vacation getaway in upper Michigan, where you can mingle with lion shifters, bear shifters, wolf shifters, witches, vampires, and many more supernatural creatures."

The visuals shift to people snorkeling in a crystal-clear lake, the water so pristine it looks otherworldly. Then, a lavish restaurant where a witch in a flowing gown conjures a flaming dessert, delighting the diners.

"Imagine swimming in crystal-clear lakes, fine dining under the stars, exclusive tours of supernatural areas, and high-class nightclubs where you can party with your favorite shifter," the announcer's voice drips with allure.

The scene changes to a vibrant nightclub. A DJ with glowing eyes spins records while a group of werewolf's dance under pulsating lights. It's intoxicatingly surreal.

"Wintermoon is a once-in-a-lifetime experience," the

announcer promises. "Book your trip now and create memories that will last forever."

The commercial fades, and regular programming resumes. A sense of longing still lingers.

I groan, returning to my task. We both know we'll never afford Wintermoon. That place is for the wealthy. I'm more likely to meet a supernatural in Downtown Detroit.

"I'm going to take my girls there one day," Angie says, hope in her eyes. She often talks about getting a chef position on the tourist island.

It's hard to believe it's been only ten years since supernaturals emerged after the pandemic. Their arrival uncovered centuries of hidden lore. Ancient texts, guarded by supernaturals, are kept in Wintermoon, and the lore on human territory is only rumors and speculation online.

Wintermoon's creatures keep to themselves, venturing out only for business. They've turned the Upper Peninsula and surrounding islands into their domain, with Mackinac Island as a tourist destination. They have a treaty with our government to prevent war—one I doubt humans would win.

I don't follow much of the lore, just bits and pieces. What I do know is their law about claiming fated mates. Government officials worldwide signed a treaty never to break it.

According to their Goddess Fate, every supernatural has a fated mate. *You can't take a mate from a mate.* Fate won't allow it. When a supernatural finds their fated mate, you get dragged off to Wintermoon, whether you like it or not, and no law enforcement will intervene.

Angie pours herself a glass of milk and chuckles as she takes a sip. I already know what she's thinking.

"What I'd give for one of those big shifters to pack up me

and my kids and haul my ass off to Wintermoon. You know they worship their women there, right?" I roll my eyes and focus on untangling the lights.

Sure, I've heard the rumors, but I've also heard the horror stories. The humans they claim disappear into Wintermoon and are never seen again. You're basically a prisoner to those creatures. Is that really a way to live? At least I have a choice here... for now.

I don't know what's happening with my government, but women's rights are slowly fading away, one Supreme Court case after another. The hostility of men and the rise of misogyny are starting to scare me. I don't know what that means for me, but I know it's not good.

As much as I don't want to admit it, Angie has a point. She doesn't like it here. Would I rather be stuck dealing with this dating pool or be fated to a supernatural who will ensure I'm provided for and protected? I don't believe in love. I don't think love gets you anywhere in this world. If it did, why would my mother be so quick to give me up to the system? I look up at the television screen, relieved to see a movie trailer. I desperately need something to pull me from my thoughts.

There's always something about seeing those ads for Wintermoon that puts me in a slump. Maybe it's because I live in southeastern Michigan, and I know I'll never see Wintermoon, Mackinac Island, or any of the surrounding small islands the supernaturals now occupy. Mackinac Island is the only space reserved for humans, but unless you find employment there, this destination is solely reserved for the rich. A one-day entry ticket alone is five thousand dollars. Who has that kind of money?

I've seen people go bankrupt just to take the once-in-a-lifetime trip. This place has practically put Disney World out of business, as it's a real place where dreams come true. I'm just a CNA. With my income and the rising cost of living, I'm sharing an apartment with my best friend Tiffany and barely saving.

"Are you still buying lottery tickets?" I ask.

I watch Angie as she eagerly nods in response to my question.

"You know I am!" she shouts back, her enthusiasm unmistakable. I can only sigh in response.

I think I've bought maybe two lottery tickets in my life. The odds of winning are like hitting the mega millions jackpot. Everyone buys these tickets, and the winning ratio is even worse since it's open to the entire world. Wintermoon has a weekly lottery, offering two winners an all-expenses-paid trip to the Island. Each ticket costs five dollars, and they announce the numbers on Sundays. I stopped trying; it feels like throwing money away.

Angie murmurs, "One day, Tami. One day I'm going to get on that Island and finally be free," her eyes glued to the television screen. I smile at her, amused by her daydreaming.

Living on Wintermoon means escaping the laws of the human world. It's said to be a peaceful place, but they don't let just anyone in. Mackinac Island offers humans a taste of their paradise, but those who get to live permanently on Wintermoon are rumored to experience true peace and serenity—like the Garden of Eden.

What a life that must be!

2

Kane

I stand on the front porch of my cabin, the crisp air biting at my skin as I take a bite from an apple. The sound of deer running through the forest reaches my ears. I consider hunting, but I'm saving that for tonight's patrol.

My cabin sits on the border of Wintermoon, surrounded by Lake Michigan and Lake Huron, within sight of Mackinac Island. My job is to patrol and ensure no intruders breach our security, which hasn't happened in years. Life has been dull, and I could easily leave this post, but I stay. I don't want to return to my village in Wintermoon. My brothers, Levi, my alpha, and Micah, have found their fated mates.

After a thousand years under the curse cast by the Bailey witches, I understand why they're reveling in their happiness. But it eats at me. Watching them find peace and start families while I wait for fate to bring me my mate is torture.

It's been ten years since the curse lifted, and life is

adjusting to a new normal for supernaturals. During the curse, without our fated mates, shifters couldn't procreate or age, trapping us in loneliness. Vampires lost their heartbeat, becoming soulless creatures feeding on blood and sleeping.

Witches turned cold and bitter, many falling into black magic. A thousand years of this drove most of us to madness. I often wanted to stop existing, but my brother Levi kept faith in our Goddess and King Amir's prophecy that the curse would lift, and we'd find our mates on our land.

The curse is gone, we have our land, but where is my mate? I grin at the black cloud of mystical smoke forming at my porch steps. It's Kade, a vampire-witch hybrid, turned by King Amir the night we lost the Great War.

Despite it being against Fate's law to turn a witch into a vampire, King Amir broke this rule, believing it was part of Fate's plan. He said Kade was destined to unite supernaturals in harmony, and so far, she's done just that.

A thousand-year-old Viking, she can be a real pain, but I love her. I love all my supernatural kin. We've been through a lot together, united in our goal to protect Wintermoon from radical humans intent on destroying our land.

She appears from the smoke, her teleportation always grating on my nerves. Every shifter hates teleportation; it makes us sick for days. The smoke lingers as she stands before me, dressed in her sheriff's uniform, smiling warmly. Kade has a motherly aura. She's spent time with every supernatural pack, pride, clan, and coven, building relationships during King Amir's slumber. Known as "*Mother Kade*," she helped establish this land with her brother Damon and the Master Coven.

We first settled in Mid-Michigan, in a small town called

Snowbush Falls. As our population grew over the decade, tensions rose between our Master Coven and the humans.

We struck a deal to take over the Upper Peninsula and the surrounding islands. We're still building, but the land is plentiful, and the seclusion is worth it.

"I think this seclusion is turning you into a recluse," Kade says, her bright blue eyes locking onto mine from the porch steps. She glances around, her gaze shifting between my cabin and the work shed. Stuffing her hands into her pockets, she gives me a motherly look. Her long blond hair flows over her shoulders and back, a mix of braids and curls that reflects her Viking roots.

"I'm fine here, Kade. You don't need to keep checking on me," I snap, tossing my apple into the forest. I leap off the porch, landing a few feet in front of her. Kade is tall, but I tower over her with my shifter height. She doesn't flinch, step back, or blink at my imposing presence.

"How will you find your fated mate if you're hiding out here?" she asks. I roll my eyes, bracing for another lecture. I grunt and walk around her, heading to my shed. She follows as I push the door open and approach my current project, a handmade crib.

I'm much older than Kade by several centuries, but she's more powerful. King Amir's blood flows through her veins, and she's his sworn daughter. Yet, Kade is different from our King's era. She doesn't care for politics or her leadership position. She enjoys being a dutiful wife and mother to her people. Leah, her wife, is also a vampire-hybrid. While Kade focuses on Wintermoon, Leah coaches newly fated mates and helps them adjust. She's worked closely with my brother Levi and his mate, Nia, who struggled to adapt as Luna of my pack.

"Fate will pull me out of my cabin when the time is right.

I like the seclusion, Kade. Don't start today," I snap. She laughs, walking to the furniture set I've just finished. She runs her hand over the hand-carved rocking chair, clearly wanting to keep it.

My work sells well in the furniture store on Mackinac Island, but I don't care for human currency. I typically send most of my earnings to my village and Wintermoon. Most supernaturals don't care about human trade, but I understand its necessity. The human dollar keeps our land rich and well-maintained, so I deal with it.

"I could rock my grandchildren to sleep in this chair," Kade mutters, eyes filled with longing. She admires the piece, and I can't help but chuckle.

"They don't make furniture like this anymore."

"Go ahead and take it, Kade. I can have another made by morning," I say, shifting the conversation. What is she doing here? What does she want? I do my job well—no human has crossed the bridge or the waters unnoticed. Kade should know she doesn't need to worry about that.

There's no trouble in my village; I'd sense it. My connection with my brothers is strong. If Levi sent Kade to coax me back to the village, it's not happening. I'm tired of hearing the moans of my fated sisters all the time. Maybe it'll be more tolerable once I have a mate, but for now, I'd rather stay on this secluded land than listen to that.

Kade snickers and flops into the rocking chair, rocking back and forth. She's going to teleport it. *I feel bad for the chair.*

"There's a storm on the horizon, and I don't have a good feeling about it," Kade says.

"I can smell it in the air. I don't need a forecast like the humans do," I snap. She chuckles.

"I'm shutting down the bridges for the rest of the week

and I've cleared the island of tourists. That won't stop some idiot from trying to cross, but the storm's current will keep them away."

"Don't worry, *Mother Kade*," I taunt. She raises an eyebrow. "I'll do extra patrols."

"And if a human tries, send them back to human territory. Do not kill anyone," she commands. I roll my eyes.

"I'll try," I say. It's all I can promise. I don't see why she's so worried. No human has tried to sneak into Wintermoon in two years. They know where we stand.

But Kade being here means something is off about this storm. Her intuition is never wrong. I look up from my project and give her a stern nod, understanding that I need to stay alert over the next few nights.

"Alright, I'll leave you to your projects. Come onto the island after the storm and try some of Leah's famous chocolate donuts."

"You know I don't eat that," I growl. She laughs.

"Call me if you run into trouble." I narrow my eyes, but she gives me a gentle wink and teleports out of my workshop, leaving a black cloud of smoke and an empty space where the rocking chair sat. I sigh, shaking my head at Kade's ridiculousness.

I don't think we have anything to worry about. The scent in the air signals a strong blizzard. No human will be stupid enough to cross into Wintermoon in this. But then again, I've seen humans do stupider things.

Fine, let them try. I'll make them wish they never stepped foot onto our land.

3

___

Tami

I'm frazzled from sorting through all those Christmas lights, but I finished. I'm off for the next two days, and honestly, I wish I had taken more overtime, even at another house. The Christmas, season feels depressing. I have no family to visit and no reason to cook a big meal. Tiffany has family, but she hardly sees them.

I've been off for an hour and still haven't gone home. I stopped at a few stores for a bottle of wine and some take-out. My plan is to sulk in bed tonight and deep clean my apartment tomorrow. Tiffany's a mess; she creates more chaos than she cleans. I dread going back because I don't want to deal with her or her boyfriend and his friends, who have been crashing at my place more than usual.

It makes me uncomfortable. I feel like some of them have been sneaking into my room, going through my things, especially my underwear drawer.

Tiffany has a drug problem that she thinks I don't know about, and her boyfriend seems to be supplying her. It feels like he's keeping her in a drugged state so he and his friends can use her.

I don't judge Tiffany for wanting to explore her sexuality, but not like this—no way. She's being used. I want to talk to her, but not in front of those guys. I can't stay out forever; there's a big storm coming, the first real winter storm for Michigan. We'll get five to six inches here, while the northern areas get hit hard.

I make the painful drive home, park in front of my building, and turn off the engine. I climb out with my groceries, too tired to deal with Tiffany tonight. I'll just put my food away and lock myself in my room until they leave.

They usually crash at my place at night and leave in the morning. I grab my mail and take the elevator to the fifth floor, walking down the long hallway to my apartment. I can hear loud music and annoying laughs from the door, and it's already getting on my nerves. I unlock the door and step inside, only to be hit by a heavy cloud of smoke. I'm 4-20 friendly, but this is too much.

I wince when I see Tiffany on the sofa, clearly intoxicated, making out with one of her boyfriend's friends. They're about to run another train on her, and I drop my bags, unable to just sit back. I fan the smoke from my face and walk over to them, ready to intervene. This is risky; I'm no match for these guys, but I have to try. Tiffany has the power to make them leave if she wanted.

"Tiffany!" I shout, standing over them. Julian, her boyfriend, grins at me, his hazel eyes locking onto mine. He's handsome, but not my type at all. I'm not about to be community property. Tiffany breaks the kiss, still teasing him, and I can see she's into it.

"What?" she snaps, annoyed that I've interrupted. What spell is she under with these guys?

"I live here too, Tiffany. I pay half the bills and clean, just to come home to this nearly every night. Are they forcing you to do this?" Before I can finish, Julian stands up, and Tiffany laughs as I gulp, shutting my mouth.

Great, what a friend she is.

"No one gives a fuck about your contributions here. You have your room; go in it. Otherwise, mind your business," he says. I stare at him, wanting to snap back, but I don't. I may have a smart mouth, but I know better than to challenge these guys. I notice his pistol in the holster at his waist and realize my place.

Kamel, the supposed friend Tiffany's making out with pauses and grabs the remote, turning up the volume on the television screen. I turn around to see what's caught his interest.

The TV flashes a commercial, and a serious voiceover begins:

"Radical activity is on the rise. These extremists threaten the safety and rights of law-abiding supernaturals. They spread dangerous ideologies and promote violence against those who are different."

The screen shows masked protestors waving signs against supernaturals, followed by disturbing footage of vandalism and aggression.

"Their beliefs do not reflect true human values of equality, justice, and peace. If you know of any radical groups in your area, report them to the authorities."

A tip line number flashes on the screen.

"Don't let extremism take root in your community. Together, we can stop radicalism and protect the rights of all citizens, human and supernatural."

The commercial fades, leaving an unmistakable tension.

Radical groups seem to be gaining traction, and I

struggle to understand this supernatural prejudice. It reminds me of the discrimination minorities like me and everyone in this apartment have faced for so long. Can't we just coexist peacefully?

"Fuck those supernaturals!" Kamel yells and Julian laughs with him. So, they're radicals? I shake off the thought. No, they're just privileged assholes who are used to getting whatever they want. No way are they radicals.

Instead of arguing, I back down and turn away, walking back to my bags as they laugh at me. Fine. But the second I get Tiffany alone; I'm ending this arrangement.

Where the hell will I move? Rent prices have skyrocketed in Detroit because of Wintermoon. My only option is to find another roommate. I could stay at Angie's for a few months; she's offered before, but her house is full of kids and problems. I don't want to add to her stress.

I take my bags into the kitchen and start unloading them when Julian approaches, standing a few feet away, scanning my body while Tiffany resumes her make-out session.

"I'm not serving you anything. That's what you have Tiffany for. She cooks, cleans, and caters to you. I'm just the roommate whose contributions don't matter." I don't look him in the eye. He laughs and leans against the counter, his gaze heavy on me.

"You're gonna be so fun to break," he murmurs. I shoot him a glare, but inside, I feel a rush of fear. What does he mean by that?

I refuse to give him or whatever he's got going on with Tiffany the time of day. I grab my bottle of wine and a glass, trying to move past him to my room, but he blocks my way. He's big, over six feet tall with a broad build.

"So fucking feisty, I love it," he muses, looking down at me. I want to grab his beard and knee him in the balls. "I'm gonna make you my woman—my main bitch." No way. I'd rather be alone than deal with this.

I force a smile and try to get around him, but he keeps blocking my path. "Move, Julian," I say, but he doesn't.

His cologne mixes with the strong smell of marijuana, and it's both unattractive and annoying. This man disgusts me, especially since he's making a move while Tiffany is across the room.

"I'm not someone you can just pass around like a toy," I say.

"I won't let anyone else have you. You're going to be my special little plaything. Maybe I'll even put a few babies in you." He moves closer, licking his lips. "You look like the kind of woman worthy of raising my children. I've always wanted a son and a daughter. I need a woman, especially now that my parents are pressuring me to marry and settle down. You know how it is for the rich—image is every-thing," he says with a wicked grin.

"Get the fuck out of my way!" I yell. He laughs but finally steps aside. I hurry to my bedroom and shut the door behind me.

I lock it, but I'm not sure it'll hold him. I sit on the edge of my bed, staring at the bottle of wine, unsure if it's safe to drink. I could see the hunger in his eyes; he's going to take what he wants.

I set the bottle down and grab the remote, hitting the power button on the TV, but the noise outside my room makes me pause.

"Why are you being so friendly with that snooty bitch? You want her, you take her. Just like you did Tiffany. And when you're done, you pass her to us for fun," I hear one of his friends say.

"I don't know," Julian replies, "I guess this one seems a little special to me." His friend laughs loudly.

"We'll take the bitch tonight. I'll dope Tiffany up enough and drop her at the house for her first customer."

"Yeah, fine," Julian mutters, still lingering at my door. I gasp but quickly cover my mouth, searching my room for an escape.

I need a plan. I stand and start the shower, making it sound like I'm getting ready for bed. Then I rush to my closet, grab my suitcase, and stuff it with clothes and underwear. I run to the window, relieved to see the emergency exit ladder. This building has had fires in the past, and the ladders were installed to prevent casualties.

I watch my door, Julian still standing there, almost as if he's listening. I rush into the bathroom, strip off my clothes, and jump into the shower. I scrub my body quickly, then step out, brush my teeth, and run a comb through my hair. I pack my toiletries as fast as I can.

After slipping into a nightdress and leggings, I turn off the light in my bedroom. That seems to signal Julian, and he finally walks away. I spring into action, pulling on socks and boots, then grab my thick winter coat, my two bags, and my purse.

I open the window and gently drop my bags onto the balcony before climbing out, pulling the window down behind me. It squeaks loudly, and I cringe, hoping they don't hear. Thankfully, Julian and his friends are too busy with Tiffany to notice.

I pull out my phone to call the police, but I hesitate. Will it even help Tiffany? I need to go back and help her, but what can I do?

I shove my phone back into my pocket, grab my bags

with shaky hands, and make my way down the ladder. Each step is agonizing, and my fear of heights grips me. The first bag, a small carry-on suitcase, slips from my grip and clatters to the ground, bouncing on the pavement. I keep going, finally reaching the second floor. My heart races when I hear the window open above me and see Julian's head pop out.

"She's running!" he shouts, then disappears back inside.

I quicken my pace, climbing down the ladder. I nearly slip but manage to reach the first level. I know they're coming after me. I grab my bags and sprint to my car, fumbling for my keys as I reach the door. I'm shaking with fear as I stuff my bags inside and climb in.

Just as I lock the doors, Julian and his two friends burst out of the building. I start the engine and throw the car into reverse, slamming into the car behind me. I shift into drive as Julian jumps into the street, trying to stop me. He pushes through without caring if I hit him as I pull away.

I keep my eyes on the road, speeding through the city toward the Downtown police station. They're about to send Tiffany off into sex trafficking. I have to report it. I need to tell someone.

4

Kane

I feel the full moon's *pull* through my workshop walls, my mind drifting to past hunts with my pack. I shut down my workshop, put away my tools, clean up, and turn off the lights. Stripping out of my clothes, I prepare for patrol. The weather alarm blares into the night, warning humans of the coming storm.

Stepping out naked, I immediately shift into my wolf form, giving my wolf control. He sniffs the cool air, digging his claws into the ground, readying his legs, then darts into the forest at full speed. The crisp night air fuels our desire to run. Even at this speed, his vision is clear, and he maneuvers through the forest easily.

My wolf pauses, hearing a small herd of deer nearby. His senses awaken, eager for the hunt. He lowers his snout, follows their scent trail, and takes off, picking up speed. The scent grows stronger, mixing with the fresh smell of falling snow. His paws pound the frozen ground, each stride powerful and deliberate. The forest rushes by in a blur. Snowflakes cling to his fur, but he shakes them off, focusing on the drumming hooves ahead.

We reach the top of a small rise and see them: a dozen deer, their muscles rippling under thick winter coats, eyes wide with fear. They notice us and sprint, hooves skimming the ground. But we're faster, built for the hunt. My wolf angles left, cutting into their path, forcing them toward denser trees. The deer scatter, but we target a young buck, slower, perhaps weakened by winter. His heart pounds, a primal rhythm driving us forward.

The buck leaps over a fallen log. My wolf follows, muscles coiled and ready. The forest closes in, the trees swaying gently in the breeze. Snowflakes thicken the air, but his eyes stay locked on our prey. We can almost taste victory.

He pushes harder, breath coming in rapid puffs of steam. The buck glances back, eyes wide with terror. That split-second hesitation is all we need. My wolf launches forward, jaws snapping shut around its hind leg. The buck stumbles, a strangled cry escaping its throat, and we tumble to the ground in a flurry of snow.

My wolf pins the buck down, his teeth sinking into its neck. The metallic taste of blood fills his mouth. The struggle is brief. Life drains from its body, and soon it lies still. The forest falls silent once more. We stand over our kill, chest heaving, snowflakes melting on his fur.

The thrill of the hunt rushes through us, but we can't linger. The snow is falling harder now, with the blizzard's full force still to come. He tears into the buck, taking what we need, then leaves the rest for the scavengers. Nature's cycle continues, even in Wintermoon.

With our hunger satisfied, we resume the patrol, senses

on high alert. Wintermoon is our home, and we must protect it. The snow muffles the sounds of the night, but he catches the faint rustle of leaves and the distant call of an owl. We move through the trees, a shadow among shadows, scanning for any sign of intruders.

The forest is dark, with patches of moonlight breaking through. Each step is quiet but accompanied by the subtle sounds of the night. My wolf is relaxed but alert, muscles tense under his fur, fueled by the excitement of the hunt. We move steadily through the trees, the cool night air a sharp shift from the warmth of our kill behind us.

As we approach the border of Wintermoon, where Lake Michigan and Lake Huron meet, the forest thins. The water stretches out before us. The sky is clear, with stars above and the moon shining bright above us. My wolf sits at the edge, his paws sinking into the soft earth, eyes focused ahead.

My mind drifts, imagining her beside us, her presence soothing our tired spirits. I picture her laughter, her eyes reflecting the moon's glow. We would show her the beauty of this place and share the wonders of the night. We would sit together, wrapped in each other's warmth, as the world around us fades away.

A thousand years. A millennium of waiting, enduring the curse those Bailey witches cast on all supernaturals. One Bailey witch from this generation saw the light, went against her bloodline, and lifted the curse. But reality is harsh. The curse may be lifted, but the scars remain. The Bailey witches' betrayal is a wound that time hasn't healed. My wolf growls again, the sound echoing through us both, a reminder of the lingering pain and anger.

He shifts restlessly, a low growl rumbling in his chest.

Memories of those dark days and endless suffering linger. We howl into the night, a mournful call that echoes across the water. It's a plea, a cry for our mate to come to us. The desperation is raw, a wound that refuses to heal.

Yet, amid the bitterness, hope remains. The night is quiet, the moon watching over us. My wolf closes his eyes, feeling the cool breeze and the scent of the lake mixing with the earthy aroma of the forest.

I don't know how much more of this we can take, not having our mate by our side. It's starting to feel like we need to leave Wintermoon and search for her, but something calls us to stay put. My wolf won't leave this area. Will our mate find us here? That's something Kade has picked up on many of the supernaturals. Fate seems to be pulling us toward our mates. This must be why we can't leave the cabin and the forest.

But the waiting feels endless, as if we're wasting too much time here waiting for her to find us. I need this woman like I need air to breathe. I want to do my duty, to provide and protect, but most of all, to love.

I want the warmth of my mate keeping me close and secure for the rest of our days. I want to watch our children grow in her belly while I ensure we have everything to make a happy home.

I've tried leaving the cabin, but we can only handle being away from the land for short periods. Eventually, we feel this strange *pull* to come back into seclusion, as if this is where we belong. Maybe we don't have a mate.

Maybe fate is trying to tell us that our job is to protect Wintermoon forever, something we will gladly do. My nieces and nephews will grow up on this land, preserving our legacy. But the pain of knowing my wolf and I may spend an eternity alone puts an ache deep within my chest.

The wind picks up, and the snowfall begins to thicken. We stay by the water for a few more hours before heading to the bridge, where we'll keep guard for intruders until sunrise. I don't think anyone will try to trespass in this weather, but if they do, it wouldn't surprise me.

5

Tami

I hold my phone out over the counter at the police station, showing the officers a photo of Tiffany. Their faces show no concern.

"Did you not hear me? I said my friend's boyfriend planned to kidnap and rape me, and he and his friends are going to sell my friend into sex trafficking. Can you please send a patrol car to my apartment?" I repeat. They ignore me.

What the hell?

These cops don't care. Why am I wasting my time asking the people I pay taxes to protect and serve me to do their jobs?

"Look, lady, we're not wasting resources because you're having a roommate squabble. Go stay at a friend's house or get a hotel room for a couple of nights until you sort things out. Now stop wasting my time before you end up spending the night here instead," one officer shouts. I lower my phone in defeat. They laugh as I turn and head for the door.

I can't go back—they'll be waiting for me. I pause at the front door of the station when I see Julian standing at the end of the street, waiting. My heart races. I turn to go back inside, only to bump into a young detective. I trip, but he catches me. His eyes follow mine as I look back at Julian, then he looks at me.

"Let me walk you to your car," he offers. I nod nervously, unsure whom to trust.

"I heard you begging the police for help about you and your friend. I'm sorry to say, but you're better off cutting your losses here," he says. The detective is clean-cut, tall, and slender, wearing a suit. He stays by my side, keeping an eye on Julian as he walks me to my car.

"Figures," I mutter. He stands beside me at the driver's side door.

"It's obvious that the sex trafficking industry goes deep within our government system. No local enforcement is going to help you. You're better off hiding out for the night, then heading to a federal agency for support. Those officers aren't going to tell you that because they don't care. Hell, they're probably waiting for that guy across the street to catch you so they can bid on you for a night. If I were you, I'd run and lay low until they forget about you," he warns. He steps back, watching as I open the driver's door and climb in. I start my engine and roll down my window, noticing Julian turn away and walk off. He's probably going to get into his car to follow me.

"So that's it? I'm on my own and my friend is lost to me?"

"You can always find a way to get a gun and handle it yourself. There's too much going on in the city for us to help you. We have bigger fish to fry with all these supernaturals popping up. I'm telling you this because I've got a sister, and I'd want someone to warn her. Get out of here before you end up on the auction block." He says, then he walks away.

I quickly put my car in drive, not knowing where to go. Thankfully, I have a full tank of gas. I pull out onto the street and immediately see the headlights of Julian's SUV following me. My hands shake as I head into Downtown Detroit, then take Jefferson Ave to I-75 north, the freeway that leads straight to Wintermoon.

Tears blur my vision as I merge onto the freeway, with Julian's SUV right behind me. I keep driving, knowing I'll eventually run out of gas. There's no way I can make it to Wintermoon on a single tank, and Julian knows that. He's going to follow me until one of us has to leave the freeway.

I've got six hours to think about what to do. When I see flashing lights from a police vehicle and Julian pulling over onto the shoulder, I thank my lucky stars. That detective must have stopped him to buy me some time. I keep going, unsure if I should take the next exit and disappear or stick to the path ahead.

I can't go to Angie's house; I'd just bring trouble her way, and she has kids. I won't do that. I might find refuge in Wintermoon, but they don't just let anyone in. What if I beg? I'll clean toilets for a year on the island if it keeps me safe from becoming a sex slave.

I don't know why, but I keep driving. After several hours, I'm down to a quarter tank of gas in mid-Michigan, some town I've never heard of. I take the exit to a truck station to refuel.

I have until Tuesday to figure out what to do before I miss work. Maybe I should find a hotel, but Julian will prob-ably be watching my job, waiting for me to show up.

I pull into a brightly lit gas station with a diner attached. I'm hungry, but my stomach is in knots, and my nerves are on edge. I park at one of the fueling stations, turn off the engine, and grab some cash from my purse.

I'm wearing a skimpy night dress, boots, and leggings under a thick winter coat. I don't exactly look like I'm coming home from a long night's work. I button up my coat to conceal my appearance and walk inside to pay for my pump.

I keep my head down as I pay for my gas, then rush out of the store to refuel and get back on the road.

"Is everything okay, little lady?"

My eyes dart up. An unnaturally tall man stands on the other side of my car. There's no doubt in my mind—he's a shifter. Our eyes meet briefly, and he smiles.

"No, I—I'm fine," I stammer. It's a blatant lie, but I need him to leave.

"You don't have to fear me, little lady. I'm not going to do anything to hurt you," he says.

I glare at him, and he chuckles, stepping back to put more distance between us. He holds up his large hands in surrender. He's dressed in a flannel shirt, jeans, big boots, and a baseball cap. This man is so big I'm sure all of his clothes are custom-made. Or maybe there are retail stores for shifters—who knows?

"Are you one of them?" I blurt out. It's stupid to ask, but he just laughs and stuffs his hands in his pockets. His face is covered in facial hair, and with the cap, I can barely see his features. He's in human form, but the human in me knows he's not your typical trucker. He's a shifter.

"Yes, ma'am, if that's what you want to call it," he replies in a husky, yet friendly tone. "Listen, little lady, if you're in trouble—"

Thankfully, my gas finishes pumping. I quickly return

the pump to the fueling station and walk over to my driver's side door.

"Nope, I'm fine. In a hurry is all. Take care," I say, climbing into my car and starting the engine. I put the car in drive and slam on the gas, speeding out of the gas station, leaving him standing there. Maybe I should have said something—he was nice and offering to help.

I don't know who to trust. I keep going, taking the ramp back onto the freeway, heading north. With a full tank of gas and two more hours before I reach the bridge, I maintain my speed and try to think of what to do. The further I drive, the messier the roads get. The blizzard picks up, and visibility drops to almost nothing. I need to stop driving before I hurt myself. There's practically no one on the freeway except me, but I keep pushing on, trying to get to the bridge as if something is waiting for me.

I drive for another three hours. The weather slows me down, burning more fuel than usual. The snow comes down so heavily I can't make out the warning signs I pass. I've been driving all night, and as the sun starts to rise, I yawn sleepily, realizing just how long I've been up.

When I finally hit the exit for the bridge, I take the ramp and drive through a small town. The bridge is closed. I can't argue my way into Wintermoon. I park and step out of the car, letting large snowflakes hit my head.

I'm exhausted, both mentally and physically. Tears stream down my cheeks. It's closed because of the weather. Stupid of me to come all this way with just a sliver of hope. I turn around and see the bright lights of an SUV approaching. In a panic, I scramble back into my car, unsure of my next move. Oh my god, Julian followed me all the way up north. This is insane.

I don't have a choice. Either I break through the barrier

and push into Wintermoon, or let this man take me. I grip the steering wheel tightly and slam on the gas, knocking over the boards blocking the bridge.

What I'm doing is dangerous. I could crash and end up in the water. But I'd rather die this way than become a sex slave. I keep my speed low, knowing whoever it is won't run us both off the bridge. My panic rises as I see the SUV following me, its lights faint through the heavy snowfall.

"Fuck! Why won't he leave me alone!" I scream, wondering why I'm so important to him. The five-mile bridge feels endless. I finally reach the little hill of the bridge, but visibility is poor. This is so dangerous. What am I thinking?

I speed up a bit as I near the end, feeling a bit relieved when the SUV's lights disappear. As soon as I hit Wintermoon's territory, my tires strike something, causing me to lose control. My car swerves off-road and flips. I scream, fear coursing through me like never before. They probably set traps to prevent trespassers.

My car rolls, my head slamming in every direction. It tumbles down into the forest, my head repeatedly hitting the steering wheel until I'm knocked unconscious.

Is this how I die? Still, it's better than the hell Julian had waiting for me.

6

Kane

My wolf snorts as we watch the car tumble into the forest, flipping until it finally stops. So, Kade was right. *A stupid human is born every day.* I want to roll my eyes when we hear a faint heartbeat. We should let the idiot die for trying to sneak into our territory.

My wolf steps onto the road but pauses when he sees an SUV drive around the trap, knowing it's there. He inhales the air, catching a shifter scent. The truck stops right in front of him, and a man jumps out, stripping off his clothes. It's Tristian, a bear shifter from the Axel Clan. He's on patrol duty on the other side of the bridge but usually stays in human form.

"This woman is running from something. I followed her until she hit the spike strip. I planned to stop her, but she thought I was someone else. I could smell the fear all over her scent." A woman? My wolf takes in the air, and the scent of her blood hits me like a tidal wave. But there's something else.

My wolf panics, and I lose control. He leaps into action, running into the forest to the car, leaving Tristian behind. My wolf arrives at the car, now upside down with its torn wheels quickly covered in snow. He slams his paw into the window, trying to reach the unconscious woman, but he can't. I try to reason with him, to shift back into human form, but he's a maniac, his mind clouded with worry. What the hell is going on?

Tristian leaps into the air, landing just a few feet from the car. He pushes my wolf aside, and my wolf starts to whimper. The woman's scent clouds my thoughts, making it hard to focus.

Tristian drops to his knees and rips the door off, tossing it into the forest. He reaches inside, tears off the seatbelt, and pulls her unconscious body out of the vehicle. Her faint breathing and slow heartbeat finally allow me to shift back into human form.

"She's alive, but barely," Tristian says, holding her close against his chest, using his body heat to keep her warm. "I spoke with her briefly in mid-Michigan. I was coasting the area, sniffing around for radicals. I picked up on her scent immediately. She's fated to someone here." Tristian's words hit me like a wave, mixed with the woman's scent, almost paralyzing me as my mind and wolf start to piece it together.

She's my mate. This woman is my fated mate.

I reach for her, but stop when Kade appears in the forest, standing before us. She inhales my mate's scent and smiles, then looks at me. Her smile quickly fades at the sound of my mate's faint breathing. She's covered in blood.

"What the fuck, Fate?" Kade grumbles, looking up at the blizzard-filled night sky. "This is not how you deliver a mate to Wintermoon." She huffs, then pulls her sleeve up and bites down on her wrist. I know what she's going to do—feed my mate her blood to heal her quickly.

The thought of Kade's blood in my mate's veins fills my wolf with jealousy. He shifts into wolf form, letting out a venomous growl. Kade pauses, raising an eyebrow.

"You have got to be fucking kidding me right now," Kade mutters, piecing it together.

"Kane, it's good you've found your mate, but she won't make it if we don't help her. Her breathing is shallow, and she's losing too much blood. Either let Kade assist or say your goodbyes. Even with Kade's teleportation, it won't be fast enough to save her." Tristian presses, and my wolf growls again before letting out a loud whimpering howl and sitting down in submission.

What choice do I have? My mate needs help. Kade bites into her wrist, breaking the skin. Snow from the blizzard nearly covers the car, but Tristian ensures his body heat keeps the snow melted around her, stabilizing her temperature. The melting snow washes away the blood, soaking her skin.

Kade presses her bloodied wrist to my mate's mouth, gently parting her lips so the blood can flow down her throat.

"I won't give her too much, just enough to help her heal. I'm not in the mood to fight your wolf. And I'm not separating another mate again. It hurt too much with Tora. Never again." Kade mutters, then pulls her wrist away. My wolf growls venomously in response. He just wants to get her home and take care of her.

My wolf winces as Kade's blood mixes with hers, but the remedy works immediately. Her breathing normalizes, and she starts to moan from the pain.

"It will take a couple of days for her to fully heal, but you have to—" I don't let Kade finish. I shift back to human form and snatch my mate from Tristian's arms, cradling her against my chest. I want her to feel my warmth, not his.

Tristian and Kade exchange a look but stay silent. I turn away, leap into the air, and land hard on the street. I take off running through the forest, heading for my cabin. If I had stayed any longer, Kade would have tried to teleport her to the town hospital, which would drive me insane. No, she stays with me.

Within minutes, I reach my cabin, where Kade is already on the porch, waiting. I carry her up the steps and kick open the door, rushing her to the fireplace. I gently lay her down and start removing her clothes. Kade, holding a suitcase and a purse, glares at me.

"Kane, put on some clothes. If she wakes up to a naked shifter over her, how do you think she'll react? And Tristian said she was running from something." She sets the suitcase down and rummages through the purse, pulling out a wallet.

"Tamera Lovington," Kade announces. Her name sends a warmth through my body.

Tamera... I repeat her name in my mind, eager to hear her voice.

"Kane!" Kade's shout snaps me back.

"Alright!" I reply, standing and reluctantly stepping away. I head upstairs, grab a t-shirt and sweatpants, and quickly dress. I gather clean towels and hurry back downstairs. Kade has removed her sheriff's jacket and is starting to undress Tamera. My wolf growls, not wanting Kade to touch her, and I throw the towels to the floor.

"Get a pitcher of hot water. I'll clean her up, check her wounds, and then I'll leave. Not before." I stride into the kitchen, fill a bowl with hot water, and return to Kade, who starts washing Tamera's skin.

My mate lies before me, her skin a deep mocha, smooth and radiant. Her full lips are set in a straight line, slightly glossy. She has a strong facial structure with high cheekbones and a firm jawline. Her long, wavy hair falls in dark waves around her shoulders, framing her face. Each feature blends seamlessly, creating a look that is both powerful and beautiful.

My eyes trail down to her full breasts, curvy frame, wide hips, thick thighs, and long legs. An urge surges through me to run my tongue over her body, but I haven't looked into her eyes yet. Kade looks back at me with a glare, sensing my arousal.

It's hard to ignore the fact that my dick is at full attention, pre-cum already leaking from the tip. My wolf screams for me to breed her, to claim her, to make sure no one else can take her from us. I turn my body away from her, open the front door to my cabin, and step out onto the front porch, letting Kade finish cleaning the blood from her body.

As I wait, it hits me—I haven't prepared for my mate's arrival. There's no food or proper clothing for her. I thought Fate had abandoned me, but she was positioning everything for the right moment. I look up at the cloudy morning sky as heavy snow continues to fall, silently thanking Fate for ending my purgatory.

7

Tami

I roll onto my side, my face pressing into the pillow. When did this stiff bed get so comfortable? I yawn hard and stretch, memories from last night hitting me like a freight train.

Climbing out of my window, down the emergency ladder, driving through the city, begging the police, taking I-75 north, losing control of my car, flipping off the road. My eyes snap open.

I sit up, my vision clearing. This is not my room. Panic sets in as I look down at my clothes. I'm wearing a night-dress, not the one I had on. My hand flies to my forehead, recalling the impact of my head hitting the steering wheel.

I should be in pain, or worse, but I feel fine—better than ever. The light of a setting sun peeks through the curtains. How long have I been out? Who saved me?

I scan the enormous bed and the large room, fully furnished and nicely decorated. Dressers, nightstands with lamps, everything is unfamiliar.

Where am I? Who changed my clothes? Even my panties are different. I hear heavy footsteps approaching the door. Panic rises. I slide off the bed, my legs wobbly, and drop to the floor, hiding under the bed.

My hands curl into fists. I bite down on my lip, nearly breaking the skin. My body shakes as the footsteps stop at the door. It creaks open. My eyes widen at the sight of massive chocolate-toned feet stepping in, each step heavy, shaking the floor.

The footsteps stop, and a low unnatural growl escapes the creature as it sees the empty bed. I gasp, clapping my hand over my mouth, holding my breath as the footsteps move closer. Tears well up as the figure turns, its heels right at the edge of the bed. It sits down on the mattress.

"Tamera," he says, his voice thick and rough, "either you come out from under the bed, or I lift it and pull you out myself."

I sigh, my body trembling at the sound of my name. It's a shifter. How much trouble am I in? He groans, not moving from the bed, but I can hear his irritation.

"You don't have to hide from me, Tamera. I don't want to hurt you," he says. "I brought you something to eat. And I'd like to check your wounds to make sure you're healing. You were on the verge of death when I found you."

I swallow hard and start to crawl out from under the bed. His large hands grip my waist as soon as I'm halfway out. I yelp. He lifts me like I weigh nothing, my feet dangling. He plops me onto his lap, and I find myself staring straight into his eyes.

I gasp.

His skin is a deep brown, enhancing his strong features. His hair is short and neatly trimmed. A messy beard frames his chiseled jawline. He has a muscular, well-defined body with broad shoulders.

The man's eyes are a striking green, almost like emeralds, with no pupils. They look unnatural, a dead giveaway that he's not human. He's wearing a green plaid shirt, unbuttoned over a snug white tee. His jeans fit well, emphasizing his solid build.

My mouth falls open.

He frowns slightly and cups my chin with his large hand, examining me closely. He smells like the forest—pine and fresh wood. I relax a bit. His hand is rough against my skin as he tilts my face, checking me over with focused eyes.

"You're healing well," he says. His breath smells like mint and pine, making me feel light-headed.

"Wha—what?" I stammer, staring up at him. He smiles, showing perfect white teeth. His canines are sharp, more pronounced. I swallow nervously.

"What were you running from, Tamera?" he asks, pulling me from my daze. My name brings back memories, always spoken with irritation. I push against his hard chest, but it's like pushing steel.

"It's Tami," I snap, trying to free myself. He doesn't let go, just stares at me for a moment, then smiles.

"Finally," he says, pleased. He chuckles. "I suppose Tami will do for now, but I'd prefer to call you my little kitten. You're feisty; I can smell it on you." I push at his chest again, and he laughs.

"You are not calling me your little kitten. And I'm not feisty," I snap, pushing at him again. "Now will you let me go, please? I'm fine."

He lifts me from his lap and places me beside him on the edge of the bed. Turning, he pulls a tray full of food onto his large lap. I quickly climb off the bed, my legs still wobbly as I steady myself. He glares at my sudden movement.

"Get back in bed, kitt—I mean, Tami," he says, correcting himself. "You still need to rest. Your body hasn't fully recovered yet." I shake my head and scan the bedroom for my belongings. He must have retrieved them from my car since I'm in a different nightdress from the one I wore the night before.

"Where are my things? How bad is my car? I need to find my phone to call my insurance company," I say, looking around the room.

His hand grabs my wrist, yanking me back onto the bed. I land roughly on my back, the mattress bouncing under me.

"What the hell!" I snap, trying to sit up, but he pushes me back down.

"I said, your body needs to rest." His dominant tone makes me stiffen. The last thing I want to do is anger this man. As soon as he feels my body relax against the mattress, he removes his hand from my belly. I sit up slowly, scooting away from him. He places the tray in front of me.

"I didn't know what you like to eat, so I had Kade bring a little bit of everything," he says.

"Who's Kade?" I ask, grabbing a slice of toast and realizing I'm starving.

"She's the sheriff of Wintermoon."

"So, the sheriff knows I'm here. Why am I not in town or a hospital? I shouldn't be here in this cabin—" He raises his hand to stop me.

"The best place for you to be is with me," he snaps. I shut my mouth and look at the tray of food. It's overloaded with pancakes, bacon, eggs, hashbrowns, and toast. Next to the plate are eating utensils and two glasses—one filled with orange juice and the other with milk. I grab the milk and chug it down.

"There are some things we need to discuss," he says. I finish the milk, place the glass back on the tray, and wipe my mouth.

"What is your name?" I ask.

He smiles. "My name is Kane—I'm a wolf shifter of the Zorah pack." His green eyes lock onto mine, staring into my soul.

I don't understand why I feel so drawn to this mysterious shifter. It's as if I was meant to be here.

So strange.

8

___

Kane

Tami stands out as strong-willed and self-sufficient. Her feistiness makes it clear she'll provide healthy and strong pups. Her olive eyes captivate me, making this thousand-year wait worth it. My desire to breed her is overpowering; my body aches to release my seed into her.

I run a hand over my face and sigh. Acting on instinct won't make her a happy mate. I need to know her better first. Times have changed; supernaturals now strive to assimilate with humanity.

Questions flood my mind, but I don't want to overwhelm her. What was her life like before Wintermoon?

Does she have family to contact? Eventually, I'll need to take her into town to register at the sheriff's station. Registration will keep her off the missing persons database. Wintermoon is her home now. She'll spend the rest of her days here with me.

She's devouring her food, clearly starving. Has she been

skipping meals? Not under my watch. I want to tell her to slow down but hold back.

"I'm sorry," she says, her scent satisfied. "I didn't mean to scarf down my food like that."

"There's nothing to apologize for," I tell her. She should be scolding me for not finding her sooner. "Tami, you blew through our barricade in a dangerous winter storm. Then you hit the spikes, something I'd expect from a trespasser. You were clearly running from someone yesterday. Who?" I ask, approaching the subject again. She tenses up at my question.

I pull the tray away and place it at the edge of the end table. We need to talk. She doesn't understand she's mated to a shifter. It's time to explain who she is to me and what this means for her. I expect an adjustment period. I don't know what she's been through.

Her scent is still muffled; Kade's blood lingers in her system. My wolf will not claim her until it fades.

I'll use this time to get to know her better before my primal instincts take over. Because, oh my god, this woman looks delicious. I try to keep my eyes off her breasts, but they keep wandering there.

"How much trouble am I in?" she asks, and I narrow my eyes. Trouble?

"You aren't a trespasser, Tami."

"Tristian, a bear shifter, spoke to you at a gas station in mid-Michigan. He picked up your scent and knew right away that you were fated to someone here. He was following you when you broke through the barrier and hit the spikes, flipping your car. He said you were already running from something when he found you. Who?" Her eyes widen at my words.

"I'm mated to a supernatural here? Who?" Her voice

rises with the question. I smile, showing my teeth. She starts to piece it together, her mouth snapping shut as she bites her lip.

Her initial shock almost feels like rejection, but then her scent changes. It's sweet and musky, blending with her natural smell of fresh apples. I shift on the bed, adjusting my shirt to hide my reaction. My wolf wants to claim her, to see our pup growing in her womb.

"Oh," she says, accepting the information. Over the past ten years with the Master Coven, moving from Snowbush Falls to Wintermoon, I've seen many rejected mates. Human women today are strong and independent, like queens without enough worthy kings.

"I—I…" She's at a loss for words, but there's no fear. Her curiosity makes me uneasy. The scent of her arousal drives me wild, but I hold back the urge to offer her relief. Now isn't the time. She needs to adjust.

"What does this mean for me now?" she asks, touching her lips. I sigh and stand up, turning to face her. Her olive eyes look up at me, pleading silently. Another wave of her arousal hits me; I clench my fists and bite my lip.

"It means you have to stay with me. It might be hard to accept now, but in time, you'll understand that your home is with me." She just stares, not resisting.

"We retrieved the few items from your car. It's totaled, but we had it towed to our repair shop. I don't think it's worth fixing. I'll take you into town once the storm clears…"

"I know what it means to be mated." She moves closer to the edge of the bed. "But I have a life in Detroit. I…"

I cut her off. "You mean the life you were running from when you got here?" I raise an eyebrow, feeling a pang of rejection at the thought of her leaving.

Tami will never understand the longing I have for her to

be by my side. Her human mind can't grasp the time gap. I've spent over a thousand years enduring this curse—unable to age, love, or procreate. I've waited all this time for her.

I don't care about her past life because her life is meant to be with me. She can run if she wants; I'll follow her to the ends of the earth. I see the hurt in her eyes from my statement, and I regret making her sad. My words hold a truth that bothers her—a truth she won't reveal. She doesn't know or trust me, and I understand her position. I just wish it didn't hurt so much.

"So that's it? I'm your mate, and I'm stuck here. Like a prisoner?" she asks, and her question fuels my anger. I want to punch a wall. She thinks this is a prison? The only prison is the life she's lived without me. I grit my teeth and take a sharp breath, trying to calm myself. I don't want to yell at her.

"Tami, the only prison was the one I endured for over a thousand years—a life without you. If you want to mourn your past life, I'll give you that. But don't call me your prison. You haven't even tried to get to know me yet."

"I—I didn't mean..." I grab the tray and walk out of the bedroom, slamming the door behind me. She needs time, and rightfully so. This is an adjustment for both of us.

I head downstairs to the kitchen to clean up her meal, then go over the groceries Kade and Leah delivered. I need to figure out what to feed her next. I've been living like a nomad, surviving on fresh meat from hunts and apples from the orchard.

My eyes pause at the bowl of fresh apples—it finally dawns on me why I love them so much. My body had already memorized my mate's scent before she was born. I fell in love with the scent of apples and their sweet taste right after the Great War. The freshness and sweetness of the fruit comforted me as I dealt with my loss—the loss of not knowing my mate.

It's odd because apples no longer appeal to me now that she's here. Keeping her secluded in this cabin away from the town isn't helping, but I can't bring myself to take her out. I want her to stay here with me, alone, and so does my wolf.

I pull the tablet out of the kitchen drawer, scowling at it. I hate these electronic devices and how humans depend on them now. Leah, Kade's wife, put a magical protective cover on it to prevent me from cracking the screen.

I tap on the device, and the screen lights up. I open the YouTube app and start searching for recipes. Visual aids on how to feed my mate are my only hope at this point.

Hopefully, I don't ruin dinner.

9

Tami

One Week Later

I pace the living room floor of the cabin, thinking about how to talk to Kane. I've been stuck here for a week, and the storm has finally passed.

My hair is a tangled mess, and it badly needs washing. I packed in a hurry and only packed some light toiletries, a toothbrush and some soaps along with clean underwear and pajamas. I need real clothes.

Kane has been mostly wonderful, though he has a temper. He feeds me and tries to bathe me, which I strongly resist.

He eventually gives in to my demands for privacy, and I do feel protected with him. But I look like a cavewoman now, and while Kane doesn't seem to mind, it's driving me crazy.

Kane spends most of his day in his work shed, leaving

me alone in the cabin, bored and irritated. Whenever I ask to go into town, he gets grumpy. Otherwise, he's sweet and loving. Why is he keeping me here?

"Enough! I need to do something!" I shout in frustration. I grab my coat and boots, open the front door, and step outside. The biting winter air hits me, and I shiver. I zip up my coat and carefully make my way down the snowy steps, my boots sinking into the snow. I head toward the workshop. When I arrive, I push the door open and find Kane standing right in the doorway, glaring at me. I jump at the sight of him, his green eyes blazing.

"It's freezing! What the hell are you doing?" he growls. I step around him, knowing his bark is worse than his bite. His tone is harsh, but his touch is always gentle.

"I need to do something!" I snap. He turns to face me, a small smile playing on his lips, as if amused by my frustration.

"I need stuff! My hair is a mess. I've been wearing nothing but pajamas all week. I'm bored out of my mind sitting in that cabin with nothing to do. Not even a book to read, just waiting for you to feed me, try to bathe me, and hold me all night until I fall asleep!" I point a stern finger at him. "You will take me into town so I can get some supplies. I can't walk around looking like a ragdoll all day."

He chuckles and gently pats my head. "I like your hair this way, natural."

"Even women in your time had a comb. I'm using my fingers!" I growl at him. He laughs and walks over to his worktable. My eyes scan the shed, taking in the beautiful hand-carved furniture.

"Alright. I'll take you into town tomorrow for supplies. Now, please go back into the cabin where it's warm," he says. I ignore him, unbuttoning my coat and sliding it off my shoulders. He slams his hammer down on the table, letting out a low growl.

"Tami," he grumbles, but I cut him off.

"There's nothing for me to do in there while you're in here working. Can't I just sit in here with you for a little while? It's lonely without you in the cabin." His face softens at my words, and he walks around the table, grabbing my coat and pulling it back over my shoulders. I sigh, feeling defeated because I know he's about to send me back to that lonely cabin.

I squeal when he grips my waist and carries me over to the table, gently sitting me down beside his current project, a small dollhouse.

"Stay next to me so you stay warm," he commands. I nod quietly. His focus returns to the dollhouse, carefully nailing the doors onto it.

"You made all of this?" I ask. He smiles briefly at me before going back to work.

"This dollhouse is for my future niece. My Luna is expecting the first child of our pack. It's a girl," he says proudly. I smile at him. He's such a sweetheart, always proud of his family. He talks about his pack, the village, and how he and his three brothers have endured so much together.

"Why do you stay here when you could be with your family? From your stories, you all seem so close." He sets the dollhouse down and stares at me for a moment. I can see the wheels turning in his eyes. He's going to make me talk. *Damn it.*

"Why won't you tell me about your family?" he asks. I shrug.

"I don't have a family, Kane," I say, not meeting his eyes. "My mother gave me up when I was five. She dropped me at my grandmother's house and never came back. My grandmother raised me the best she could, but she passed away when I turned thirteen. I spent the rest of my teens bouncing from foster home to foster home until I turned eighteen. Then my social worker cut me a check, and I was on my own after that. I made friends with a girl named Tiffany while in the system, and we were roommates before..." I trail off, unable to finish.

I feel like I abandoned her by not going back for her. She doesn't know that Julian and his friends are using her, preparing to sell her into sex trafficking, and I just left her. I should have fought for her, but something told me to run.

I felt this *pull* I can't explain it—something drew me to drive up to Wintermoon, to seek safety here. And when I look at Kane, I'm slowly starting to understand why. I feel safe with him, safer than I've ever felt in my life.

Kane walks around the table, his large warm hand gently cupping my face, lifting my eyes to meet his.

"There you have it, I'm a broken mate," I say, but he shakes his head.

"You'll never be alone again, Tami. That, I promise you." I close my eyes, leaning into his touch. What is happening to me? The more time I spend with Kane, the more I feel drawn to him. When he left this morning to come here to his shed, I felt a sense of loss. I hated it. I haven't left because I'm bored. I'm still here because it hurts to be away from him.

"I think you're finally starting to feel the *pull*," he announces, bringing me back to focus.

"*The pull*?" I manage, closing my eyes again and leaning into his touch as he gently massages my cheek.

"That's right, you don't know much about the lore of my people," he murmurs. I moan from his touch. The feel of him, his warmth, the softness of his touch—it's like I'm falling under a spell I can't escape.

"*The pull* is an invisible band created by our Goddess Fate. It's magical, binding us together. The pull keeps us from separating, and it becomes painful when fated mates are apart for too long. You'll feel it even more once we've claimed each other."

"Oh," I whisper, intoxicated by his nearness.

"I cannot wait for the night I get to claim you." He moves closer, his face just inches from mine, his sweet breath brushing against my lips. My eyes roll back, my entire body heating up, feeling like it's on fire. My breathing quickens, and my heart races. He closes his eyes and inhales, then a low growl escapes him as he presses his forehead against mine.

"I can smell your arousal, Tami. You've been torturing me with it for a week now. I need to mate with you," he says, his breathing quickening. I swallow, leaning back against the table.

"You need me, Tami. You need me to ease the ache between your legs. Do you want me to take care of you with my mouth or my dick?"

"Oh, my god," I moan, letting my head fall back against the table. He moves with me, gently pressing his lips against my forehead.

"Give me permission to eat your pussy, Tami," he murmurs, his lips moving to my cheek. His hands start to explore my body, heightening my arousal even more, but he pauses when his hand reaches my belly and my stomach growls, completely ruining the moment.

One thing I know about Kane for sure, he treats making sure I'm well-fed like it's his top priority. I've watched him stop whatever he's doing at the sound of my hunger pains just to feed me.

"No, wait!" I say, gripping his shirt as he pulls back, but it's too late. The mood is ruined. He scoops his arm around my waist and lifts me effortlessly from the table.

"I've waited over a thousand years for you, Tami. I can wait a little longer to have you. You need to eat, and I'm going to feed you," he says. I groan, letting my head rest against his chest as he carries me out of the work shed.

10

_____

Kane

I f I don't breed my mate soon, I think my dick is going to explode. The smell of her arousal slamming into me over and over again was enough to nearly send me over the edge.

I'm not going to fuck her on the table like she's some piece of meat. She's worth more than that to me. And I want her comfortable, especially when it comes to experiencing her heat for the first time.

I hate that my supernatural history was erased from humanity after the Great War. If it were the old days, Tami would have been properly prepared by her village.

Based off her heavy scent of apples, her bloodline is from Kenya, or Southwest Cameroon. Her people understood the laws of Fate well, and some of the women from their villages could tell early on when a woman had been chosen by Fate.

But my woman is lost to her people thanks to colonization and her history wiped clean from her bloodline. She doesn't understand any of this, why she felt the urge to risk her life in a dangerous blizzard to get to me. She needed safety and her body knew I could provide that for her.

As I rummage through the kitchen for pots and pans to cook her something to eat, I scowl at her for being so self-conscious about her hair. She unravels the long braid from the thick, natural curly texture, then runs her fingers through it.

I understand she's uncomfortable with not grooming herself to this westernized standard. She thinks I don't care about how she looks, but what she can't see for herself is her natural beauty that's radiating from her.

Her once straightened hair is now thick with beautiful long tight curls that fall just beneath her shoulders. She's a vision in her natural state. She doesn't need all of those products and heat added to her hair.

As a male, I know it's best to keep my mouth shut in situations like this. I'll just keep putting my foot in my mouth. I want my mate to be happy with me, not pissed off and irritated by my presence. She grins when she notices me pull the tablet from the drawer and start to search for cooking tutorials.

Tami uses the tablet while I'm working and it's odd, she hasn't tried to access social media at all during her time with me. She simply browses information on the lore of Wintermoon. She won't find much on the internet, other than rumors and speculation.

I'll take her to the Master Coven where our libraries are located if she wants to know more about our people. But that's not happening until we get better acquainted with one another. It's already going to be a painful trip onto the island so she can grab the supplies she needs.

The scent of her arousal is thick and filled with need. I

don't think we are going to make it through the night. Her body is screaming for me to breed her. But her mind... is hesitant.

"I can cook my own food sometimes," she mumbles, running her fingers through her hair. I smile, ignoring her as I pre-heat the pan and start to warm some pre-cut turkey, along with two slices of bread.

"It's my job to serve you, Tami. And it makes me happy to do so. So please, could we not fight about this today?" She lets out an adorable huff, then meets my eyes, giving me what I want.

"What am I supposed to do as your mate? Just sit around here and look pretty?" She mutters. She's bored, sitting in this cabin all day.

I haven't exactly made efforts to make it comfortable for her. Partially because we won't be staying here. When we move back to my village, she will be busy getting to know her pack sisters and I don't want to share her right now.

I think humans like to call this the honeymoon phase...

"Is that a problem, Tami?" I ask her.

I'm so sick of these formalities. She is my mate; I should be allowed to call her whatever I want. She's my woman, my Goddess, my sweetheart. Her mouth flops open, a bit surprised by my candidness, and she quickly snaps it shut, blushing. I can see the heat rising in her cheeks.

"You said something about a curse earlier. A curse was broken so you could find me. What curse?"

The memories of enduring, waiting, and longing flood back to me and I shudder. I look up at her with a soft expression as I recall how agonizing it was to wait for her.

"It's a very long history, but I'll give you the shorter version. It started with the Great War. A witch fell in love with a human king that was not her fated mate. She went against Fate's law, killing her fated which is punishable by death. Amir, our King, placed a bounty on her head to make her pay for her crimes. The human king forged a war to protect his love, but humans are no match against supernaturals. To protect humans, the witch along with members of her coven cast a spell on supernaturals, one that she knew would make us lose our will to fight. It was a curse, preventing all supernaturals from finding their fated mates. Shifters lost their ability to age and procreate, vampires became soulless monsters, and witches were stripped of emotions. The curse not only affected us, but the witches who cast the spell."

I finish preparing her meal and place the plate in front of her, a turkey melt with two pickles, and a glass of apple juice, then walk around the counter to sit beside her at the attached bar. She looks at me with a pained expression. I smile at her and gently stroke her cheek. She doesn't need to be sad for me.

"I lost my family in the Great War. My parents and most of my pack. The only living members of the Zorah pack are me and my three brothers. Levi, my oldest brother, became alpha of our pack by default due to his age and strength. My other brothers, Gabriel and Micah, are with him in our village. Levi found his mate first, then Micah. Now me." She closes her eyes and leans into my touch.

I want to make love to her so fucking bad right now, she's the only cure for this sadness I feel from the ache of waiting for her for so long. But I can't take her like this.

"Only Gabriel is left without a mate now, but I'm sure his suffering will end soon. I think Fate drew me here. It was the reason why I couldn't bring myself to take a break from patrolling the border. I think my wolf knew. We were waiting for you to come to us." She opens her eyes and stares right at me, those beautiful olive eyes are always so easy to get lost in. She closes her eyes and sighs for a moment, her expression pained and full of frustration.

"Before I flipped my car off the road, it was just a simple night of me getting off work. Tiffany, my roommate, started spending time with the wrong crowd. I think she was into drug use. Julian, her boyfriend cornered me in my kitchen. He said I would make a great mother for his children." She jumps at the growl that escapes me.

Another man intended to breed my mate? And live? Ha! I'd feed on his corpse for a week, then raise his children as my own. I draw in a breath to calm myself. I'm not trying to scare her from talking to me. But the only children that will be filling her womb will be from my seed alone.

"Please keep going," I push, and she nervously shakes her head at me.

Fuck! I try not to growl out my frustration as I watch her grab her sandwich and take a bite of it.

"Is this boyfriend, the man you were running from? Is he what brought you to me?" She doesn't have to answer me. I can see the answer written all over her face.

"I don't want you to kill anyone for me. I've heard the horror stories, of what happens when humans try to interfere with fated mates of Wintermoon." She says and I stifle a chuckle.

Oh, she doesn't know the half of it.

"Will you tell me his full name at least?" I ask her, and she shakes her head.

Doesn't matter, I'll find his scent. I could smell another man's scent on her panties when I unpacked them. That asshole has been playing with her underwear without her permission. My wolf howls inside of me, wanting vengeance. Feasting on his flesh seems like the perfect compromise.

"I think I'd like to save the rest of this conversation for the police once you take me into town. I want them to help me with this, not you." She says and I narrow my eyes at her.

What? Why doesn't she trust me to handle this? I could make him go away within less than twenty-four hours. I just need his scent, which I partially already have.

It's faded from me over the past week, but it's imprinted in my memory. Once I catch whiff of it again, I'll be able to complete my hunt.

"Why is that?" I ask, trying to keep my tone neutral. She takes another bite of her sandwich and gives me a stern look.

"Because I don't want that asshole to be the reason I lose you. Let the police handle it, and we can continue getting to know one another. Alright?" I give her a gentle nod, but my wolf is beaming with pride.

I want to snatch her into my lap right now and kiss her silly. She's not protecting that asshole. She's protecting me.

Oh, we are most definitely not going to make it through the night without me breeding her.

11

Tami

I don't know why I said that to Kane. I've only known him a week, but the thought of losing him makes my chest ache. *This pull* between us has taken hold of me.

Kane seems deeply focused on learning more about me, so I steer the conversation toward my work as a CNA. It works, shifting his attention away from probing about Julian.

I don't want to talk about Julian. Something tells me Kane will go after him. What kind of trouble would he get into?

No, his life was fine before I came into it with my baggage. I'll handle this on my own. Human law enforcement didn't help with Tiffany. Maybe Wintermoon's police will. It's worth a try. She could be mated to someone here.

Kane tells me about his pack and their long history as carpenters and architects in their village in Kenya. He describes how he built and furnished a hut for me, preparing for his fated mate. But everything changed when King Amir called him to aid in the Great War.

We talk for hours, more than we have all week. As I get to know him better, I start to understand him. We move from the kitchen to the sofa. The sun sets, and a fire in the fireplace warms the room as the winter night sets in.

"The curse ended during the pandemic," Kane says, "when a Bailey witch went against her coven and broke it. I heard it was due to fascism, which seems rampant among your people now. I'm thankful the curse ended, but I can't forget what the Bailey witches took from us. I can't forgive that."

I look into the fire, unable to find words to calm him. What would I do in his shoes? I'd hold a grudge, maybe worse. I don't know the Bailey witches, and I don't hate them. I'm just happy to be here. I stretch and yawn. Kane moves suddenly, lifting me into his lap, his hand touching my cheek.

"Time for bed, baby?" he asks.

The pet name catches me off guard, and I smile. We lock eyes, staring deeply, almost as if we're touching each other's souls. My body heats up, arousal surging through me as the warmth of his presence envelops me. I want him to kiss me.

"Tami," he breathes, inhaling deeply.

I know he can smell my arousal. I don't want to hide it. I see the struggle in his eyes, the effort to control his urges. He's always so gentle, but I crave something rougher, darker. I don't want him to hold back.

"I want your mouth," I say, addressing his earlier question from the workshop.

"Ah, fuck!" he growls, and then he gives in.

His lips crash into mine, making the world around us fade away. The intensity of his kiss melts me into him, each touch igniting sparks through my body. My fingers grip the back of his head, pulling him closer, trying to fuse us together.

Kane's kiss is overwhelming, each movement filled with hunger and devotion. I can barely breathe, my heart pounding in my ears.

When I finally break the kiss, gasping for air, he doesn't pause. His lips travel down my neck, planting soft bites, his teeth careful on my skin. The sensation sends shivers through me, my skin tingling where his mouth has been.

Lost in the haze of lust, I hardly notice when Kane picks me up. It's not until my back hits the bed that I realize he's carried me upstairs to our bedroom.

The firelight from downstairs casts a warm glow, shadows dancing on the walls as Kane's eyes meet mine. I gasp at their green glow, knowing his wolf is present.

I lay back, surrendering, letting him explore my body. His mouth and hands are everywhere, moving from my neck to my breasts, pulling them from my dress, licking and sucking each nipple.

Waves of pleasure wash over me, and I moan, my hands gripping the back of his neck, pulling him closer. His hand moves down, gripping my leggings and panties, pulling them off.

"Kane," I breathe, but he's lost in his desires.

His mouth stays on my breasts, sucking and biting my nipples. He rips my nightdress off with one pull, leaving me completely nude. He looks at me with pride, making my heart flutter.

"So, fucking perfect," he mutters.

Before I can respond, he moves down my body, kissing me until he's between my legs. He spreads them wide, grips my hips, and pulls me to the edge of the bed. He closes his eyes and inhales deeply, his face inches from my pussy. The tension is intense, every nerve in my body alive with need.

He kisses along my inner thighs, and I shiver, my hands gripping the sheets. When his tongue finally touches me, I gasp, my body arching off the bed.

The sensation is electric, a blend of pleasure and relief. His long, slow strokes send waves of pleasure through me, building until I feel like I might explode.

His tongue circles my clit, and I cry out, my nails digging into the sheets. He is relentless, his mouth worshipping me with a devotion that makes my head spin.

The heat inside me builds, a tight coil of pleasure ready to snap. When his tongue flicks over my clit again, I lose control, my body shaking as I come apart, crying out his name.

He doesn't stop, his mouth continuing to work me through my orgasm, drawing out every last bit of pleasure. When I finally come down, trembling and spent, he looks up at me, desire darkening his eyes. He moves up my body, kissing me deeply, and I taste myself on his lips. It's intoxicating, and I kiss him back with all the passion I have left.

He pulls back, looking down at me with a possessive gaze that makes my heart race.

"Mine," he growls, and I nod, speechless. He kisses me again, softer this time, a promise in his touch. His hands roam over my body, gentle now, as if memorizing every curve and line.

"Kane," I whisper, my voice shaky. He looks at me, his expression softening.

"What do you need, Tami?" he asks, his voice rough with emotion.

"You," I say simply. He smiles a warm, genuine smile that makes my heart ache with love.

"I'm yours," he says, and I believe him.

I want more. I need to feel him inside me. He quickly removes his clothes and climbs into bed with me. My eyes widen at the sight of his length. *Dear god, that is not going to fit in me.* He grins, pulling me on top of him.

"I know you need more, Tami," he says, and I groan, unsure how I'll handle him.

"I'll give you a little more, then you'll sleep. I'm not breeding you tonight," he tells me.

"Wait—what?" I manage, then gasp as he lifts me over his head, positioning me over his face.

"Ride my face until you come," he commands. With a swipe of his tongue across my slit, I fall onto his face, his palm smacking my ass, forcing me to grind against him.

"Use me, Tami. Take what you need from me."

I grind against his face, matching his thrusts as he buries his tongue inside me.

The sensation is overwhelming, his tongue reaching places I didn't know existed. My body moves on its own, hips rocking back and forth, my hands gripping the headboard for support. Each stroke of his tongue sends waves of pleasure through me, and I can't help the moans that escape my lips.

His hands grip my hips, guiding my movements, and I feel the heat building inside me again.

The pressure is intense, and I know I'm close. Kane's tongue flicks over my clit, and I cry out, my body trembling. He growls against me, the vibration adding to the pleasure, and I lose myself in the sensation.

"More," he growls, and I can't deny him.

I ride his face harder, my thighs shaking as the pleasure builds and builds. His tongue is relentless, and when he sucks my clit into his mouth, I come undone. My orgasm crashes over me like a wave, and I cry out his name, my body shaking with the intensity of it.

"Kane!"

He doesn't stop, his tongue still working me through my release, drawing out every last bit of pleasure.

When I finally come down, breathless and spent, he lowers me back onto the bed. I lay there, panting, my body still trembling from the aftershocks.

Kane moves up my body, his eyes dark with desire. He kisses me deeply, and I moan at the taste of myself on his lips. He pulls back, looking down at me with a possessive gaze that makes my heart race.

He chuckles at my pout when he pulls away from me and scoops his arm under me, lifting me off the bed and repositioning me so that my head is against the pillow.

Then he grabs the blanket folded neatly at the edge of the bed and covers me with it. I want to pleasure him the same way he's done for me, but I can't. My body is too weak to move. He gently brushes his fingers over my sweaty forehead.

"I want you to sleep so I can take you into town in the morning. I want you to get all the supplies you need because you won't be leaving this cabin for a while." My heart quickens at his words, my hand cupping his face, pulling his lips to mine, his beard tickling my skin.

He keeps the kiss brief, pulling away and holding me close against his chest until I fall asleep.

12

Kane

The Next Morning—Mackinac Island

I don't think I'll be able to get my dick to soften until my wolf is sure she's been properly bred. Last night keeps replaying in my mind: the taste of her, the way she rode my face, her ass bouncing against my chin. I wanted her to stay there until I suffocated.

I don't drive. I know how, but as a wolf shifter, I prefer to travel on foot. It's just a preference, but now that I have Tami, maybe I should think about getting a vehicle. I doubt she'll enjoy this old-fashioned way of traveling.

For now, I set her on the bed of the trailer and pull it up the small hill to the road that leads to the docks. It takes us about fifteen minutes to get there at my pace.

Once we reach the docks, I lift her off the bed and we wait for the ferry to Mackinac Island. It's the only way to get there. I have a small trailer, just big enough for her to fill with supplies to last us the month.

She fidgets with her messy hair, looking uncomfortable in her thick coat, boots, one of my oversized flannel shirts that fits her like a dress, and a pair of leggings. At least she's warm. She can restock her closet with fresh clothes and underwear while we're in town.

"I'm a Michigan native and I've never been this far up north, not even before your people settled here," she murmurs, staring at the water as the ferry comes into view.

There are two ferries that cross this area: one for shifters and the other for human tourists. Tami looks nervous, but she has nothing to fear. She's home now, with me.

"You're just twenty-five, Tami. You were only fifteen when supernaturals first revealed themselves." She smiles at me, but I can see the memories of her past surfacing in her eyes. It frustrates me. I can't stand seeing her unhappy.

"You're home now, Tami, with me. Let's focus on our future," I tell her. She nods and leans into me.

No other shifters seem to need to travel on the ferry today, which is typical. On Wintermoon, we have our own shops and recreation facilities, but I'm taking her to the island to avoid my brother, Levi. If I see him, he'll command me to take Tami out of the cabin and into the village with the rest of the pack. It's where she belongs, but I need this seclusion with her for a little longer.

The ferry finally arrives. I help her board, grab the trailer, pull it onto the ferry, and then help the shifters running the docks prepare to sail. Tami watches from a bench, her eyes following the two shifters chatting with me. I know them well.

One is Tika, a bear shifter from the Ridge Clan, and the other is a lion shifter from the Lorra pride. I smile when she gets offended that they refuse to meet her eyes as they greet her. It's a sign of respect. Both of them are mated and work the ferry to keep busy while their human mates work on the island.

I dread even thinking about my mate working. It's not necessary for our mates, but we allow it to give them some autonomy. Judging by Tami's strong-willed stance, I have a feeling we'll discuss her working on the island, which I don't want to think about right now.

After a thousand years of waiting for her, the only thing that would make me happy is her lying on her back with her legs spread wide, waiting for me to breed her over and over.

Goddamn, Tami better pray my dick calms down once I breed her for the first time tonight. My wolf is getting anxious, tired of waiting. He's ready to claim her. Having a taste of her last night did not help matters.

Once the ferry sets sail and I'm sure the trailer is secure, I sit beside her on the bench. The warmth of my body keeps her warm during the twenty-minute ride to the island. She rests her head on my shoulder and takes a quick nap during the journey.

During the ride, I focus my thoughts on providing for Tami, not just my desires. What does she need? I know she enjoys books, music, and movies. I'll need to get a television and mount for the living room, plus a couple of bookshelves.

When we arrive, Tami watches in awe as I pull the trailer effortlessly off the ferry. I take her hand and walk with her into town. Her eyes widen at the sight of the shopping center, a full block of various shops.

Tourists pull out their phones, treating me like a zoo exhibit, while Tami decides which shop to enter. She chooses a women's boutique first. I follow her inside, feeling proud as she browses through the clothing racks. She looks back at me, biting her lip.

"Some of this stuff is expensive," she says.

I stop her. "I want you to fill the trailer with whatever you want, baby." I gently run my hands through her curly hair, noting it needs moisture. I make a mental note to wash it for her tonight. "Don't worry about money. I've got it."

She narrows her eyes at me. "Are you rich or something?"

I chuckle and shrug. "Human currency is nothing to me. But I've made a small fortune selling my handcrafted furniture to humans over the years. There's a small furniture shop here in town that I help keep stocked. I prefer the money to go into my village."

She puts a finger to her lips, staring at me. "Oh," she says, turning back to the racks. "I'm just a CNA. I was barely making ends meet, but I loved my job." She grabs a few more dresses in her size. I step in front of her and take them from her hands so she can grab more.

"None of that matters now, Tami. You have me now, there's no need to worry about money. I will always make sure you are well taken care of."

She ignores me, walking over to the underwear section. My eyes immediately travel to the sexy lingerie on display. Tami giggles when she catches my gaze, and I see the playful glint in her eye.

"Do you want me to grab one for tonight?" she asks, then her eyes narrow and she points an accusatory finger at me. "Don't even start, Kane. I know we won't make it through the night without fucking."

My eyes widen, and for the first time in my life, I blush. I want to point out one for her to wear, but I don't.

It doesn't matter; it's just fabric, and I'm going to shred it from her body to get to her skin. She grabs a black night-dress from the display and hands it to me, giving me a playful wink. Then she loads up on underwear, watching in awe at the counter as I pay for everything.

I gaze at her as she examines the new clothes. "So, I'm mated to a rich shifter. This is great," she says, her voice dripping with sarcasm. She reaches for the bags, but I stop her. "Just change into something we bought," I suggest. "You'll blend in better with the tourists."

OUR NEXT STOP is the pharmacy. It has all the toiletries she needs. As we approach, Leah, Kade's wife, steps out of the bakery, flour dusting her face and hair. She spots us and immediately throws her arms around Tami, catching her off guard.

"Finally, Kane's let you out of the cabin for a bit," Leah says, looking at me. She beams a warm smile at Tami, who stiffens when she notices Leah's fangs.

"Don't worry, Tamera. I'm a friendly vampire-witch hybrid. I help with the bakery sometimes, but mostly, I assist newly fated mates in adjusting to Wintermoon. You seem to be doing well," Leah says, her smile genuine.

"Please, call me Tami," she replies, managing a stiff smile.

Leah is stunning with her big bright brown eyes, tan skin, and long wavy dark brown hair pinned up in a messy bun, streaked with flour.

I appreciate the work she and Kade put into making Wintermoon thrive for supernaturals. We've never had a community like this before, but it aligns with the prophecy that one day supernaturals will rule the earth.

Another Great War looms, but this time, nothing will stop us.

"We'll chat soon, Tami. Finish your shopping," Leah says. Tami looks to me for approval. I pull her into a gentle kiss, then hand her some cash and urge her to go ahead.

She walks off, glancing back at me occasionally as I stay behind to talk with Leah. I can see the lecture coming. As soon as Tami enters the pharmacy, Leah turns to me.

"It's been over a week, and I don't see a claim mark on either of you. What the hell is going on?" she demands.

I sigh and roll my eyes, stuffing my hands in my pockets. Tourists gawk at us, snapping photos and taking videos, but we ignore them.

"And why is she here with human tourists? She should be on the mainland, getting to know your pack. What are you doing, Kane?"

"My wolf doesn't want to share her just yet, and neither do I. For the record, I'd like to get to know her a little better before I claim her like some wild animal," I snap back. Leah smiles at me, understanding.

"I always knew you were a sweetheart. Your poor mate won't know what hit her when you finally claim her, and you are going to change into a monster when you do." I groan, not wanting to have this motherly lecture with her, but I continue out of respect.

"It will happen tonight. As for taking her before the Zorah pack, I'd like a little more time," I tell her. She places her hands on her hips.

"Take Tami to get registered before you leave, and I'm not stopping Levi if he decides to show up on you to find out why you're hiding your mate away. That's pack business." She gives my chest a gentle pat, then walks back into the bakery.

Leah's words hang in my mind as I focus on the pharmacy, blocking out the chatter of the tourists. I can hear my mate's heartbeat as she shops for what she needs. What kind of monster am I destined to become when I finally claim her? My wolf is unruly and restless.

We've been isolated for too long. I don't want to share her now; will I really be able to share her once the claiming process is complete? I know I can't keep her locked away in the cabin, even though my wolf yearns to hide her from the world.

I've got some growing up to do, otherwise it's going to destroy my mate.

13

Tami

He just handed me a wad of cash, like it was nothing. This has to be over three thousand dollars. I stuff it in my pocket and grab a basket, filling it with items.

This store doesn't have much for a Black girl, but I get excited when I find a couple of jars of edge control. I grab them and place them in my cart.

I load up on shampoos, conditioners, deodorants, soaps, and lotions—everything I need to feel human again. I add a new blow dryer, hair straightener, some makeup, perfumes, and several combs and brushes.

As I head for the checkout, Kane catches me off guard, taking the heavy basket from my hands.

"That was my first time seeing a vampire and a witch," I say. Kane smiles and shakes his head.

"No, you actually met her wife, Kade, first. She helped clean you up and nurse your wounds, but you were unconscious. After we finish here, we're stopping at the police station to get you registered. And there's something you wanted to discuss with Kade about the man chasing you..."

I cringe. "You have to promise me that you won't—"

"I don't compromise when it comes to protecting you, Tami," he cuts me off. His tone is final, making me nervous. I try to pay for the items with the cash he gave me, but he pulls out his card and pays.

"What did you give me the money for then?" I ask. He smiles and shrugs.

"I like taking care of you. Is that a problem?" he retorts. I snap my mouth shut because what can I say to that?

He walks me out of the store, and I'm just happy I finally have the supplies I need so I can take care of myself. I pause by the trailer as he loads the bags onto it. My eyes scan the island, and I wince at the tourists gawking at Kane.

Yes, he's big and beautiful, but he's mine. A wave of jealousy hits me, and Kane's laugh only heightens my irritation. I keep forgetting he can smell my mood shifts. I glare at him, then turn my eyes back to the town, trying to rid myself of jealous thoughts.

There are so many beautiful women staring at him, and he's got a thousand years of experience compared to my mere twenty-five. I feel out of his league.

My mood shifts from jealousy to insecurity, then Kane jumps down from the trailer and gets right in my face, towering over me.

"Knock it off, Tami, or I'll take you back right now and prove you have nothing to worry about," he warns.

I bite my lip nervously and nod. He walks over to the trailer, closes it, grabs my hand, and we walk through town. As we walk, I take in the view of the town.

The streets of Mackinac Island in winter are covered in fresh snow that shines in the pale sunlight. Victorian houses line the narrow cobblestone streets, decorated with wreaths and lights. The colors of the houses show through the frost.

Horse-drawn carriages on sleigh runners glide quietly over the snow, leaving tracks behind. The air smells of pine, and I hear laughter and conversation.

People bundled in scarves and hats walk by their breath visible in the cold, snapping photos of Kane while keeping their distance.

We walk for a few more minutes before arriving at a small police station. Kane opens the door for me. The last time I walked into a police station, I was turned away. I glance up at Kane nervously.

"Come on, I need to get you registered and hear about the jerk who ran you out of town," he says, smiling at me. I groan but step inside, needing to get this over with.

A woman in a sheriff's uniform stands up from her desk. Her bright blue eyes and long blonde hair, along with her height, remind me of those Viking women from my favorite TV shows. She seems familiar, and then I see her name tag: Kade.

So, this is Leah's wife. She's stunning, but I wince when she smiles, revealing sharp white fangs.

"You look a lot better than when I found you a week ago," Kade says. Her eyes scan both sides of my neck, narrowing in suspicion.

"Um, is everything alright? Why haven't you claimed her yet?" Kade asks, looking at Kane. Kane groans and walks over to the desk, pulling out a chair for me.

"Can you register my mate, please? I'm not having this discussion with you." Kade snickers then looks at me.

"You seem to be handling Kane's wolf well. Kane likes seclusion, but that will change now that you're here. Command his wolf to let you out of the cabin, or you'll be stuck there. You have a lot of power, Tami. Use it," Kade says, winking at me before returning to her desk. I follow her and sit in the visitor's chair Kane pulls out.

Kade holds up her sharp nails, sighing in irritation. "I hate typing with these. I could trim them, but they grow back in minutes."

"Before we start, there's something I need help with," I say. Kade leans back in her seat, waiting for me to continue.

"When I arrived, I was running from someone. My roommate's boyfriend. I overheard him planning to kidnap me with his friends. They were talking about selling my roommate into sex trafficking. I tried to go to the police, but they turned me away."

I look up as a man enters the station. He's wearing a full suit, looking elegant and wealthy. He stomps his shoes on the rug, shaking off snow, then walks over to stand beside Kade. He has bright green eyes and short blonde hair.

"This is Damon, Kade's brother and sheriff of Winter-moon," Kane explains. I give Damon a nervous smile, and he smiles back, flashing his fangs.

"Welcome to Wintermoon, Tamera," he greets me. "It's no surprise the police turned you away. They actively work with sex trafficking rings. Give me his name and I'll look into it." Damon says, and Kade smiles at him.

"Another trip to Detroit. I could use a fresh kill," she says. I wince at that.

I look back at Kane, who smiles at me, waiting for the name.

"Julian," I say, "Julian Blackmore." Kade and Damon share a knowing look, as if they're familiar with the name.

"I can't make any promises, but we'll try to help your friend," Kade says. I let out a sigh of relief and nod to them both.

"Thank you. Her name is Tiffany Woods." I look down at my hands, fidgeting. "We weren't exactly close; we were on different paths. But I still care about her, and we've been through a lot. If you can just make sure she's okay... I feel guilty for leaving her behind."

"We will do what we can, Tamera, I promise you."

"It's Tami," I correct them. Kade pulls a set of forms from her drawer and places them in front of me.

"We already have you in the system, but I need you to sign these forms. It's legalities to ensure no one can try and take you from Kane," Kade explains. I shrug and take the pen from her hand.

"I've been alone for a long time. No one is going to come for me," I say. Kane places his hand gently on my shoulder. Kade collects the forms after I finish signing and beams a smile at me.

"You're officially a daughter of Wintermoon. Well, you were regardless of these forms... but politics..." she mutters, handing the paperwork to Damon. Kane immediately grabs my wrist and pulls me from the chair into his arms.

"Before you leave, Kane. We need to have a discussion," Damon says, setting the papers on the desk. Kane pulls away from me, his eyes burning with fury. There's a change in their color.

"You can't keep Tam—Tami in the cabin forever. She needs to be with your pack," Damon says, stepping from behind the desk and approaching Kane. My eyes widen as I glance down at Kane's hands, which are morphing into monstrous claws.

Fear grips me. I've never seen him react this way. I gasp, taking a step back and covering my mouth as Damon draws nearer.

"I understand your pain, Kane. I'm still waiting for my

mate and I'm much older than you. You want to keep her close, you don't want to share her, but we are a tribal people. You can't exile yourself or your mate from the village," Damon says calmly.

"You cannot take her from me," Kane spits out. Kade stands up from her chair and positions herself between them.

"That's not what's happening, Kane," Kade says, placing her hand on his chest. "We are only talking. Now please, calm down. You're scaring your mate." Kane looks over at me, and his hands immediately shift back to human form.

"I'm taking my mate home. That's enough for now," Kane declares.

Kade smiles. "Leah already stocked your trailer with groceries. It should last your mate a month. After that, you're officially banished from the island until you take Tami to your village," Kade announces with a wicked grin. Kane growls at her but she stands firm, unfazed.

Kane walks over, grabs my hand firmly, and pulls me out of the station. I glance back at Kade and Damon, who wave at me.

I hope they can help Tiffany.

14

Kane

We get back to the cabin just after sunset. Tami heads straight for the trailer, ignoring my protests, and starts pulling out several bags. She carries them inside and runs up the stairs to our bedroom without a word. Since we left the island, she hasn't spoken to me. Earlier, her fear was clear—a fear I caused.

I start unpacking the trailer, taking most of the bags to our room. She's already in the shower when I get there. Maybe she's so angry she just wants to go to bed. But she needs to eat first. I won't let her go to bed on an empty stomach.

After dropping the bags, I head back downstairs to the kitchen. I finish unloading the trailer and put away the groceries. Then, I start preparing her dinner.

The silence between us is agonizing. I wish I could hear her thoughts. Her scent is conflicted. Is it because of me? My wolf is disappointed for losing control. The thought of losing her is enough to drive me crazy.

I'm not even thinking about being intimate right now. I just want her to stop being upset with me. She stays upstairs for another agonizing hour. I finish her dinner, but the plate starts to go cold as I pace the cabin floor.

Should I serve her upstairs? She's not sleeping. I smell burning hair. Why is she taking so long?

I run my fingers through my curly hair, feeling the urge to be with her growing stronger.

Just as I start to head for the stairs, I pause. Relief washes over me as I hear the bathroom door open. She descends the stairs, each step making my heart pound.

When she reaches the bottom, my breath catches. She's wearing the sexy nightdress from the boutique. It barely covers her, stopping just below her hips.

The thin straps hold up her beautiful breasts. She has a light coat of makeup and a barbell nose ring. I didn't know she had a piercing. I run a hand through my beard, taking her in. She's straightened her long curls, which cascade down her shoulders and back.

I'm going to sweat those curls right out of her hair tonight.

She smiles and approaches me slowly, giving a playful twirl to show off. She's looking for my approval; I can smell it. I love the dress and what she's done for me, but it won't last long once she finishes dinner. My body aches for her, and my need is almost unbearable.

I grip her wrist gently. "Come on, baby. It's time for dinner."

I guide her to the bar and lift her into a chair. She lets out that adorable squeal I love to hear. I sit beside her and slide the cool plate over.

"I can heat it..." I start, but Tami is already digging in, clearly starving. I watch as she devours the chicken, broccoli, and rice I prepared.

"I'll take cleaning duty," she mumbles between bites. I laugh. *The only thing she's doing tonight is riding me.*

The first night will be rough for her since she's not used to my size, but she'll adjust. She's not a virgin; I can smell one other man on her. I want to kill him for touching her, but I hold back. The scent is old; she was young when it happened.

Killing him would make me a hypocrite. My sexual history is far longer than hers. I spent centuries in purgatory, not knowing if I'd ever find her. I filled the void with other women, but I can only love Tami. I was made for her. She wants me tonight, and she'll get her wish.

She eats like she's starving, and I'm mad at myself for forgetting to feed her while on the island. She finishes quickly, washing down her meal with the juice I prepared. She sits back, rubbing her full belly. My eyes drift to her hand on her abdomen, aching for the day she's pregnant with our child. I have to know.

"You said you were running from Julian because he wanted you to have his children," I say. She narrows her eyes.

"I don't want to talk about Julian while I'm trying to seduce you," she mutters, making me smile. She sighs and meets my eyes.

"He's sketchy, a drug dealer involved in sex trafficking. He's wealthy and doesn't even need to do it; he just likes it. I want children, lots of children, just not by him." She pauses, looking at her belly. "Is that something you want? I don't know what it's like to have a family. I spent most of my life facing rejection. When I turned eighteen, I was on my own. I got my diploma, the state paid for my CNA license, and I buried myself in work for five years." She pauses, mistaking my silence for rejection.

I stand and raise my hand to stroke her cheek but pause when her eyes follow my movement. I sense her curiosity.

"I saw your hands shift at the police station. That's the first time I saw your wolf. You never shift in front of me. Why?" she asks. I pull my hand back, but she catches it, smiling as she places my palm against her cheek, closing her eyes, and leaning into my touch.

"I'm unsure how you'll react to seeing me like this," I admit. I hold up my free hand, partially transforming it into my wolf form. Her eyes widen as my human fingers shift into thick, black claws. I curl them into a fist, then open and close it. Surprisingly, she doesn't smell of fear, only curiosity.

"Will I become like you?" she asks, reaching for my claws. I pull my hand away.

"It's not that I don't want you to touch me, Tami," I say, gently moving my other hand from her cheek. "My claws are sharp. I don't want you to get hurt." I shift back to my human form, then grip her hips and lift her from the chair.

I scoop her up and carry her to the sofa, sitting down with her in my lap. She wraps her arms around my neck, and I close my eyes for a moment, savoring the embrace.

"You won't become a shifter when I claim you, but you'll get stronger, more durable. Your aging will slow down. You'll experience changes while carrying our children, but those will fade after you give birth. I'll be with you every step of the way. You'll never be alone again, baby." I reassure her.

She shifts on my lap, straddling me. My dick stiffens in my jeans, aching with need. I exhale, trying to maintain control. My hands rest on her hips, my body reacting as if it's my first time. I'm no virgin, but this is my first time with my mate, something I've longed for.

"You're nervous," she murmurs, meeting my gaze.

"Yes, very nervous. I'll remember this moment for the rest of my life. I want it to be special," I tell her. She smiles and presses her lips to mine. Her kiss is tender, full of love, and it overwhelms me.

My hand moves to her lower back, deepening the kiss. My tongue traces her bottom lip, asking for entry. She gasps and parts her lips, and I bury my tongue in her mouth, devouring her. Her arousal spikes, and she grinds against me. That's when I lose it. I fucking lose it.

Any willpower I had vanishes. I need to have her now.

15

Tami

I'm know Kane is about to take me, but I don't care. I'm lost in lust, letting him kiss me until I'm almost dizzy.

One hand grips the back of my neck while the other holds my waist as he lifts me from the sofa, never breaking the kiss. I moan into his mouth, kissing him back.

Kane's lips are firm, his beard brushing against my skin and sending shivers down my spine. His green eyes, now dark with desire, lock onto mine, making my knees weak. He picks me up effortlessly, holding me as if I weigh nothing. My fingers tangle in his thick beard.

He moves slowly, each step bringing us closer to the stairs. My heartbeat quickens, a mix of anxiousness and need rushing through me.

Kane's lips move down my neck, finding the sensitive spot below my ear. I gasp and tilt my head back, giving him more access. His teeth nip at my skin, and a growl rumbles from his chest.

Before I can catch my breath, Kane slams me against the wall, his body pressing into mine, his lips devouring me until I'm gasping for air. His mouth is hot and demanding, and I'm lost in the sensation. His hand moves to my ass, squeezing while the other holds me securely against him.

He starts moving up the stairs, one step at a time, his lips never leaving mine. I wrap my legs around his waist, feeling his hard body against my softness. His hand slips under my panties, his fingers curling around the fabric. With a single powerful tug, he rips them away, leaving me bare.

"Kane," I moan, desperate. My need for him is overwhelming, crashing over me. His name escapes my lips as a plea, a surrender.

At the top of the stairs, he carries me into our bedroom, laying me down gently on the bed. I try to scoot back, but he grabs my ankle, pulling me to the edge. His eyes scan my body with hunger, making my skin tingle and my core tighten with need.

Kane lowers himself between my legs, his breath hot against me. His eyes meet mine, the connection electric. Slowly, he presses his lips against my pussy, kissing it tenderly. Then, his tongue slides out, drawing a line from bottom to top, and I cry out, my hips bucking off the bed.

"Ah!" I scream, raw and unrestrained. He holds me down, his tongue thrusting inside me, and my eyes roll back from the intense pleasure.

"I need to prime you, get you ready for me," he murmurs, his voice a low growl vibrating through me. His tongue moves quickly, each thrust sending waves of pleasure through me. My body trembles, my legs shake uncontrollably.

He pushes my legs back, spreading me wider, his tongue

hitting all the right spots. My toes curl, and my breath comes in short, sharp gasps. The pleasure builds until it snaps, and I explode, my orgasm washing over me.

Kane keeps going, his tongue relentless, pushing me to the brink of madness. My hands clutch at the sheets, my mind a whirl of ecstasy.

Finally, he pulls back, releasing my thighs. I lie there, limp and breathless, staring up at the ceiling. He stands, his eyes never leaving mine, and begins to undress, each piece of clothing revealing his muscular body.

I watch, my body still tingling from the lingering pleasure. Kane stands before me, naked, his arousal evident.

My breath catches, and I bite my bottom lip, staring at the length of his shaft. It's already leaking with pre-cum, long, thick, and stiff. I don't think it'll fit, and if it does, it might tear me apart.

"I've waited centuries to be with you, Tami," Kane says. "I'll remember this moment for the rest of my life, and not a day will go by where I don't worship you for it. You mean everything to me—my world."

"What?" I blurt out, still delirious from my orgasm.

Kane grips his shaft, stroking it as he climbs onto the bed. He wraps an arm under my waist, pulling me further up, kicking my legs apart. He positions himself at my entrance, gliding the head of his member up and down my folds. Kane moans from the sensation, then leans down and plants a gentle kiss on my lips.

"Take a deep breath, baby," he says, cupping my face.

My breath catches, and my back arches as he slowly slides inside me. He grunts and groans, and I can feel the warmth of his seed filling me, his dick pulsing against my walls. He buries his face in my neck, biting down gently but not hard enough to break the skin. He stays like that for a few moments, coming down from his immediate orgasm.

"Good, now I can last longer," he murmurs against my neck. I grit my teeth, bracing myself for the thick deep strokes of his dick, pushing in and out of me. He starts to slide in and out, each thrust sending waves of pain and pleasure.

I wince, clawing at his back, but he keeps thrusting, starting to increase his pace. His cum leaks out of me, coating my thighs and the mattress. It feels like he's slamming into my guts with each stroke.

"You're doing so good, baby. Take every inch. You were made for me," Kane murmurs, planting gentle kisses on my cheek as he continues to thrust.

His praise pushes me over the edge, and I cry out in pleasure, my walls clamping down on his massive length as he continues to stretch me.

"Kane!" I cry out, "Oh my god!" I'm panting, gasping for air, wrapping my legs around him as he continues to slam into me. He's breathing heavily, grunting, going deeper, harder, stretching my walls.

"Kane, I can't..." I cry out, my orgasm so powerful I feel like I might pass out.

"You're squeezing me so good, baby. Take all of it, take all of my cum inside you. You're going to give me a lot of babies," he grunts between thrusts. His hand grabs my nightdress, and with one pull, he rips it off, exposing my breasts. He continues to slam into me, latching onto my breasts one by one, sucking, biting, teasing.

"I can't wait to see these tits full of milk. You aren't just going to feed our pups; you're going to feed me too," he says.

"Ah!" I cry out again, another wave of my orgasm

crashing over me. I just keep coming and coming; he's pushing me to madness.

"That's it, Tami. Keep squeezing me. It's coming, I'm about to unload more of my seed into you," he grunts, pushing harder, deeper. My eyes roll back as he keeps stroking, sending me to peaks of pleasure I didn't know existed.

"Tell me you want this. Tell me you want my babies," he commands.

"I—I want your babies," I cry out, clawing at his back, desperate for something to hold onto as he pushes the orgasm out of me.

My words ignite something in him, and he slams into me one final time, pushing so far, so deep that I can feel his seed pouring into my womb, and I welcome it.

He pulls back, gazing into my eyes. There's a darkness in them, one that I haven't seen before. His wolf is starting to come out, and he's ready to claim me, make me his forever. I should fight this, beg him to get off me, but I can't. I want this; I want Kane to own me, every inch of me.

He's panting heavily, his gaze so intense as he continues to pump his seed into me, filling me up.

My body feels completely limp, and my legs and arms feel like jelly, both of us covered in sweat. My hair, which I spent an hour on, is completely damp from our intense love-making. I brace myself for what's coming next—receiving my claim mark, a scar that will stay with me for the rest of my life.

"You're mine, fucking MINE!" Kane shouts, and his teeth lengthen into sharp fangs.

My eyes widen in horror as he comes down on my neck and sinks his teeth into my flesh, breaking the skin. I scream and claw at him to stop, but he keeps drinking, blood pouring into his mouth and spilling onto the bed. He drinks until he's satisfied, then pulls back and swipes his tongue along the bite mark, sealing it with his saliva. When he's finished, he pulls back to look at me, and my eyelids grow heavy.

"Tami, baby... I—I'm sorry," he says, but darkness falls over me, and I pass out.

16

Kane

T ami's climax, mixed with a hint of her blood, lingers on my tongue. I hold her close, leaning against the headboard, waiting for her to wake up. I'm worried I might have been too rough. My wolf took over after breeding her, and I claimed her immediately. My dick still craves her, hungry to breed her again and again.

The orgasms with her are incredible. The way she took every inch, the way her pussy clamped down on my dick repeatedly—I'm addicted to this woman, like a drug.

A wave of madness washes over me. It's unsettling, and my wolf demands I lock Tami away. I can't share her with anyone. Just thinking about bringing her to my village sparks rage inside me. I don't want anyone near her, looking at her, breathing in her direction. She is mine.

MINE.

I hold her tighter, feeling her stir against my chest as her eyes slowly open. I didn't mean to wake her. She hums softly, a peaceful smile spreading across her face when she sees me. Her sleepy gaze meets mine, but then the memories of last night start to surface. Her hand instinctively goes to her neck, fingers brushing over the mark there. She looks back at me, her expression nervous.

"I'm sorry. I was rough with you," I say.

"It doesn't hurt," she replies, shifting away from my chest and sitting up in bed. "It seems to have healed already; there's just a scar left from last night." She glances down at her naked body and tries to pull the blanket over herself, but I tug it away, leaving her exposed.

"There's nothing to be shy about. You are so beautiful— so perfect." She blushes, running her fingers through her tangled hair. She pulls a lock of it in front of her face, sighing in frustration.

"I guess it's pointless to put heat on my hair," she mutters, and I chuckle. I lean forward, gripping her waist, pulling her back against me, already missing her warmth.

"How do you feel?" I ask, desperate to check on her. She shrugs.

"Alright, I guess. Last night..." she pauses, and I smile when I catch a whiff of her arousal. I thank Fate for giving me a mate with such a hungry pussy. I bite my lip, my gaze filled with lust.

I want to breed her again, my dick twitching under the blanket at the thought of being inside her. Memories of the hard strokes of my dick in her tight pussy flood my mind, making me ache with need. I see the same level of lust in her eyes. But I don't want to hurt her.

She bites her lip, climbs into my lap. Her slick pussy glides over my shaft as she removes the blanket from my lap and grinds against me.

I let out a low moan, placing my hands on her hips to try

to stop her. But she presses her lips to mine in a hungry kiss, throwing her arms around me.

My hand instinctively moves to my shaft, positioning it at her entrance. I'm hoping she'll wince—anything to slow me down—but she slides down on my shaft, her body taking me in completely. She moans with pleasure as I fill her.

"Fuck!" I groan. She rises up from my shaft, whimpering, then slides back down, taking in my full length.

"Tami, ah fuck!" I cry out, feeling myself losing control. Her strokes are slow and deliberate as if she's teasing me into madness. I grip her hips, guiding her up and down on my length, hard and rough.

Our bodies move together in a rhythm, and her breasts bounce against me as I slam her up and down.

Her moans blend with mine, each sound heightening our desire. I feel her walls clenching around me, each movement sending waves of pleasure through my body. I can't take it—I'm losing control.

I grip her hips tighter, my fingers digging into her skin, and I thrust up into her, matching her downward movements with force.

"God, Tami, you're so tight," I grunt, my voice strained as I struggle to hold back. Her nails dig into my shoulders, and she throws her head back, her hair spilling over her shoulders. She rides me harder and faster, and I feel the pressure building inside me, a volcano ready to erupt.

"Yes, Kane, just like that," she whispers, her voice breathy and desperate. Her words spur me on, and I thrust harder, deeper, feeling her walls stretch to accommodate me. She whimpers, a sound that sends shivers down my spine, and I know she's close.

"Fuck, Tami, I can't hold back," I warn her, my voice

rough with need. She looks down at me, her eyes glazed with lust, and nods.

"Don't hold back," she says, her voice a low growl. "Give it to me."

That's all I need to hear. I grip her hips with bruising force and slam into her, each thrust harder than the last. Her breasts bounce wildly, and I lean forward, capturing one in my mouth, sucking and biting gently. She cries out, her body tensing around me, and I know she's on the edge.

"Come for me, Tami," I command, my voice a low rumble. "Let me feel you."

She moans loudly, her body convulsing as she reaches her peak. Her walls clamp down on me, and it's overwhelming. I let out a roar, my body shuddering as I spill into her. The sensation is intense, pleasure flooding through me and leaving me completely focused on her.

We collapse together, our bodies slick with sweat, breathing heavily. I hold her close, feeling her heart hammering against my chest. I never want to let her go.

"I want to meet your wolf," she says between pants. "I see him creeping out here and there, but I want to see him in full." I squeeze her tighter, holding her against me.

"Alright," I say. She pulls back and starts to slide out of bed. My eyes narrow, wondering where she's going.

"Where are you going?" My question almost comes out like a growl.

"To the bathroom to pee and take a shower. I want to meet him, right now." She commands, and I moan, letting my body sink into the bed. She'll get what she wants from me, but my mind is still in a daze from the orgasms she just gave me.

I have a feeling we're going to keep going at this until my

seed takes hold in her. Her body wants to be bred, and my dick is more than willing to provide what she needs.

When I hear the toilet flush and the water from the sink turn on, I peel myself weakly from the bed to join her in the bathroom, my dick hardening at the sight of her.

This woman is going to drain me completely dry. She turns on the shower and climbs in, and I follow, pulling her into a deep kiss as she dips her head under the water.

"Are you sore?" I ask, pushing her up against the shower wall. She nods nervously, biting her lip, and I quickly step out to grab the washcloths she's set on the counter, lathering one with soap to wash her body.

"It was worth it," she blurts out, and I smile at her.

I smooth the cloth over her body, stiffening when she winces as I reach between her legs to clean her. I don't like that she's in pain. We'll have to take breaks if this is becoming too much for her.

Plus, there's also the possibility that I'll lose my sex drive once she becomes pregnant. It's a natural state I've seen male shifters fall into. As for Tami, her sex drive will increase, but I'll do everything in my power to make sure she's satisfied as long as it doesn't harm our little ones. I want her relaxed, happy, and nurturing our children.

I plant a gentle kiss on her lips, one she accepts willingly, then dip her back under the shower to rinse her off.

She wants to meet my untamed wolf. I'm worried how she might feel meeting him. He's wild and overly playful. I don't want him to hurt our mate, but the growl coming from him lets me know he's going to introduce himself to Tami whether I like it or not.

So, I guess it's best that I go along with this.

17

Tami

Kane zips my coat, grunting. He clearly doesn't want me outside in this weather. But I need to see his wolf. Last night, it wasn't Kane who bit me; it was his wolf. I need to see it again.

"My wolf is untamed, Tami. He can be overly playful and doesn't know when to stop. I want you to greet him, then go back inside. Don't play with him," he says. I narrow my eyes. He glares back, a warning that without my agreement, he won't shift. I bite my tongue and nod. Now is not the time for sarcasm.

Kane starts stripping, pulling off his clothes until he's naked. I grab his arm as he pulls off his t-shirt.

"What are you doing? It's freezing out here," I say, then realize he's a shifter. The cold doesn't bother him.

"I don't want to shred my clothes. And I'm fine with the temperature, baby," he says, leaning in to plant a gentle kiss on my forehead. He steps off the porch barefoot, standing in front of the cabin.

I watch, my heart pounding, as Kane begins to shift. His muscles ripple, bones crack, reshaping under his ebony skin. Thick, black fur bursts forth, glistening in the night air. The transformation is both mesmerizing and terrifying.

Kane's human form disappears, replaced by his massive wolf. He's enormous, twice the size of a normal wolf, with a thick, velvety coat. His bright green eyes, vivid against the black fur, lock onto mine. The predatory pupils send a shiver down my spine.

The wolf growls, a deep sound that vibrates through my chest. He bears his sharp, gleaming teeth. Fear grips me, but I remember Kane's words: *his bark is worse than his bite.* I take a deep breath.

"I know you won't hurt me," I say softly but steadily. I move down the snowy porch steps cautiously. Kane's wolf continues to growl, making my heart race.

The wolf takes several steps back, barking and growling, saliva dripping from his mouth. I move closer, holding my hands up cautiously.

"I want you to sit down and let me pet you," I say firmly but gently. The wolf pauses, confused. Then he whimpers, a soft sound, and sits, submitting.

I wonder if I can really tame such a wild beast. Slowly, I close the distance. Kane's wolf lets me approach, lowering his snout. I reach out and run my fingers through his warm, thick fur. His growling subsides, replaced by a soft, rumbling purr.

The fur feels unexpectedly soft and warm against the cold air around us. I can feel his powerful muscles underneath, tense but slowly relaxing under my touch. His bright green eyes lock onto mine, and there's an unspoken connection between us.

"You're very soft," I say, smiling.

Suddenly, Kane's wolf flips onto his back, sending a spray of snow into my face. I fall back, wiping the snow away, annoyed. He presents his belly to me. I remember how the dogs in my old foster home used to do this to show submission. I sigh and lean down, running a hand over his belly. Kane's wolf moans in pleasure.

"It's nice to meet you, Kane's wolf," I say. The wolf rolls back onto his side, watching me. I start the steps to the porch, and Kane's wolf quickly rises, moving towards me as if he doesn't want me to leave.

"Kane said I can only say hello. Now I have to go back inside. Maybe another time," I say, turning to go up the steps. Kane's wolf whimpers, and it tugs at my heart. I sigh, turn back, and see him sitting, his tail wagging.

"I never had a family. Seeing you with Kane makes me happy. At least he wasn't alone," I tell him. His wolf whimpers, and I step down from the porch to pet him. He leans into my touch as I massage his wolf's skin through his fur.

"Maybe we can play a little, but you can't be too rough," I say. His wolf snorts, seeming irritated by my comment. I chuckle and grab some snow, forming a snowball. I toss it at him, hitting his snout. He shakes off the snow while I laugh.

But his reaction isn't playful. He leaps into the air, startling me. I cover my face as he pounces, knocking me into the snow. We slide across the ground, and when I open my eyes, his tongue swipes my cheek. I grunt, pushing at him, but he keeps licking my face.

"Will you stop!" I complain. His wolf pulls back, then suddenly stiffens, sniffing the air. He starts to whimper and sinks into the snow. I sit up, confused, then notice the cut on my hand, blood pooling in my palm. I wince.

"Oh shit, I'm in big trouble now," I mutter.

Kane shifts back into human form and grabs me before I

can react. I squeal as he carries me up the stairs and onto the porch, kicking the door in. He sits me down on the sofa, grabs his clothes from the porch, and pulls them on before slamming the front door shut. I walk over to the sink to rinse the blood from my hand, which is dripping onto the floor.

Kane storms into the kitchen, his eyes blazing with fury. He looks like he wants to tear my head off.

"It was just an accident," I say, but he grips my wrist and examines my palm.

"I told you not to play with my wolf," he growls. He holds my hand up, examining the wound carefully. Then he gently swipes his tongue over the open wound. My mouth drops open as I watch it heal immediately, leaving a scar behind.

"My saliva has healing capabilities now that I've claimed you," he explains, picking me up and setting me on the counter. He presses his forehead to mine, and guilt washes over me. I didn't mean to upset him.

"I'm sorry, Kane. I should have listened to you," I say, gently cupping his face. I try to kiss him, but he pulls away.

"I should start dinner. I need to feed you," he says, moving to the fridge and taking out some thawed chicken.

I watch him for a moment, feeling a mix of guilt and frustration. "Kane, please... I didn't mean to..."

He places the bowl with thawed meat on the counter, then cups my face, pulling me into an intense kiss that makes stars flash in my vision.

"I need you to understand something, Tami," he murmurs against my lips. "I will not lose you. I cannot survive in this world without you. I've done enough of that for a thousand years." I nod nervously. He sighs, pressing his forehead against mine and gently rubbing my cheeks.

"I don't trust my wolf around you yet. When I give you a

command, I want you to listen to me. Understand? I'm not doing it to be an asshole. It's for your protection." I nod, and he sighs again, his body relaxing. He releases me and grabs the bowl, walking to the sink to wash the meat.

"I can cook my own food sometimes," I tell him again, but he ignores me.

"Go take off your coat and boots and relax by the fire. I'll call you when dinner is ready." I narrow my eyes at him and climb down, following him to the sink to protest, but a low, unnatural growl escapes him, making me pause.

I gasp and quickly turn around, hurrying into the living room, pulling off my coat and kicking off my boots. I dash to the sofa and snuggle under the blanket folded neatly on the armrest.

18

Kane

Has she lost her mind? She tried to play with my wolf. I hate myself for trusting she'd listen. My wolf doesn't know his own strength. He got excited when his mate accepted him and lost control.

I felt the way my wolf's teeth grazed her hand when he landed on her. It could have been so much worse.

We just found her. Not even a month in, and I'm already hurting her. A wave of depression and sadness hits me, but I keep preparing her meal.

I'm getting the hang of how humans cook. I've always enjoyed the meat of a fresh kill, but I know I can't feed Tami that way. I can eat human meals, but I don't enjoy them. They're just tolerable.

Tonight, I try frying some chicken for her. She watches me quietly, running her hand over the scar in her palm. Her mind seems to be racing, and I'm desperate to know what she's thinking. She's so beautiful, just sitting there, waiting for me to feed her.

I think back to how many times I dreamed of this moment. Hundreds of years, unable to shift out of my wolf form, too depressed at the thought of never having a mate and fulfilling my duty in this world. Now, here she is.

I clear my thoughts and finish the chicken. She stands from the sofa restlessly when I turn off the stove and wipe it clean. I pull out a pot to boil some rice and steam vegetables. She sits down at the bar, reaching over the counter and grabbing a chicken wing.

"For a shifter who doesn't cook for himself, you seem to be pretty good at this," she muses, biting into the meat.

"I do well with visual aids," I say, stirring the rice as it begins to boil. She takes a bite of the crispy chicken and gives me a thumbs up in approval. She looks at the bitten chicken, then back at me.

"How come you never eat with me?" she asks, meeting my eyes. I give her a gentle smile, then pick up a piece of chicken, taking the entire piece into my mouth, chewing everything down to the bone before swallowing. Her eyes widen in surprise.

"Damn," she blurts out, and I chuckle.

"I don't think you can stomach my tastes. It's not that I can't eat human food, I just don't enjoy it. I enjoy fresh meat from a hunt." I grab a glass and go to the fridge, pouring her some juice. I place it on the counter next to her.

"Shifters only drink water," I explain, pointing at the glass. "I prefer fresh water from the lake over what comes out of the pipes."

"Oh," she says. I grab a small plate from the cabinet and turn off the stove, letting the rice and steamed vegetables cool before serving her.

"I'm sorry about earlier, Kane. I should have listened to you. Your wolf is so sweet. He didn't want me to leave, and it was hard to tell him no," she says, staring down at the plate of food.

"I'm sorry for snapping at you. It's just that..." I sigh, looking ahead, trying to find the right words. "The fear that crept in when I caught the scent of your blood. I can't lose you, baby. I've lived long enough without you. I can't do it again." Her breath catches, and I smile, hoping my words sink in.

I pick up the fork from her plate and hold it out to her. She takes it, scooping up some food and taking a bite.

Tonight was a lesson. My wolf has our mate wrapped around his scheming little paw. He was reckless and overly playful. He could have hurt her. I push the thought away and focus on her eating.

My stomach rumbles, the hunger pangs settling in. It's time for another hunt, but not until she's asleep. She finishes her food and drink quickly, smoothing her hand over her belly with a satisfied smile.

"You're spoiling me, Kane. You're doing everything right. You keep my belly full, protect me, clothe me, provide shelter..." I catch a whiff of her arousal. "And the sex..." she clears her throat. I want nothing more than to take her again, but she needs rest.

"I'm doing my duty," I say, then come around the counter and scoop her up from the chair. She squeals, wrapping her arms around my neck as I carry her through the living room and up the stairs to our bedroom.

"Duty? You make it sound like a job," she mumbles.

I set her down at the edge of the bed, pulling off my clothes. I won't be with her tonight, but the warmth of my body comforts her, making her fall asleep quickly in my arms. She gulps, taking in the sight of my naked body.

"Tami, I'm a shifter. I think differently from a typical

human male. My thoughts are more... primal. When I came of age, I knew I would eventually be paired with my fated mate. My father, the former alpha of my pack, trained me to prepare for you. He taught me how to hunt, build a hut, and fight, so I could protect you. Most importantly, he taught me how to love. I yearned to love a woman the way my father loved my mother. He took excellent care of us and made many sacrifices as an alpha," I say, dropping to my knees in front of her, carefully helping her out of her clothes.

"Fulfilling my duty is not just a job to me, Tami. It's something I honor, and I'll forever thank my Goddess Fate for bringing you to me." She stares at me, speechless.

I want her so badly right now. My primal urges feel over-powering. I want her pregnant. I know my desire won't calm down until that happens.

Tami yawns and stretches as I climb into bed with her, pulling the covers back. I wrap an arm around her waist, pulling her under the blanket with me. She snuggles against my chest, her body fitting perfectly with mine.

The bond is growing stronger. Soon, she'll cling to me and want to be wherever I am. I welcome that moment.

Tami yawns again, her exhaustion settling in. "I need to find my phone or get access to one so I can call my friend Angie and let her know I'm okay. And my job—I already know I'm fired, but I need to figure out how to get my final paycheck. And then there's my apartment. I need to get my stuff," she mumbles tiredly.

I squeeze her tight against me, hating the thought of her leaving. If she needs something from her old life, I'll get it for her myself. She can't leave me. Wintermoon is her home now. She looks up and smiles, puckering her lips for a kiss. I lean in, not denying her.

Shit.

This is going to be a rough hunt tonight. The thought of Tami leaving sparks a rage in me, my canines extending involuntarily. Tami doesn't notice; she's resting against my chest, the warmth of my body lulling her into a peaceful sleep. Once I'm sure she's out, I slide out of bed. I don't bother with clothes since I'm shifting for a hunt.

I head downstairs, putting out the fire in the fireplace. My eyes drift to the coat rack where her purse is hanging. I want to dig out her phone and destroy it, but I hold back, my hands curling into tight fists.

I'm feeling myself losing control, so I quickly head to the front door and open it, stepping out onto the porch and shutting the door behind me. I close my eyes and relax as Tami's soft snores echo through the cabin.

I leap off the porch, shifting into my wolf form mid-air, my wolf's paws hitting the snow as he lands. My wolf shakes his fur, letting out a low growl, scanning the area for any potential threats before moving on. He patrols the surroundings for about an hour before darting deep into the forest for a hunt.

I try to keep my thoughts clear to avoid angering my wolf, but it's no use. I can't stop thinking about Tami and her need to resolve things from her human life. It's a normal reaction for her but sharing her isn't something I can handle right now.

My wolf pauses and slows his steps as we catch the scent of a moose. Moving carefully through the snow, the crunch beneath his paws is barely audible.

Ahead, the moose comes into view. It's a large male in its prime, with impressive antlers. The moose shifts around, searching for food but remains alert, sensing danger.

I feel the tension in his muscles as my wolf lowers his body, eyes locked on the moose. Each step is calculated and deliberate. The moose looks around nervously, its instincts warning it that something is out there.

My wolf surges forward, muscles coiling and releasing like a spring. He slams into the moose, bringing it down. The moose cries out, thrashing beneath us. My wolf's frustration reaches a breaking point, turning this kill chaotic and furious. Blood sprays across the ground, mingling with the moose's cries that echo through the forest.

I hate this. I prefer quick kills; fear ruins the taste of the meat. But I don't try to calm my wolf. I let him take over completely. He tears into the moose, shredding flesh and bone. The forest fills with the sounds of tearing, snarling, and the moose's dying cries.

Once the moose is dead, my wolf feeds, ripping chunks of meat and swallowing them whole. Blood stains the snow around us, standing out against the white landscape. When he's full, my wolf sits back, panting. He licks his nose and begins cleaning his fur, each swipe of his tongue deliberate.

As he calms down, I regain control, and the reality of our situation hits me. If we leave Wintermoon and return to Tami's human life to tie up loose ends, I risk killing a human.

My wolf is too wild to trust in a populated area. I need to ask Kade to handle Tami's belongings and pick up her final check, but I'm not sure how Tami will react to this news.

19

——————

Tami

Kane is acting so weird and it's starting to drive me crazy. Ever since I woke up and plugged in my cellphone to charge, he's been glaring at it like he wants to break it.

How can he be jealous over a phone? It's just a phone! It takes a few hours to charge, and thankfully, the screen isn't cracked.

Kane busies himself in the kitchen, watching tutorials on how to make pancakes. I join him despite his protests for me to sit on the sofa and just watch him. He's been very busy since I was sleeping. He unpacked all the groceries, mounted the television over the fireplace, and it looks like he went out for a hunt. I found some blood in the shower this morning but didn't ask about it. I'm just glad he's eating what he enjoys.

"Tami, please," he whines as I grab the spatula and flip a pancake.

"Kane, relax. There's nothing wrong with me making my own food." He glares at me, but I'm not afraid of him.

"But my duty..." I stop him before he can finish.

"I understand your duty, Kane. And you are doing a wonderful job taking care of me. But it can't just be about me all the time. Let me take care of you sometimes." I tell him, taking over the stove. He grins and steps behind me, pressing himself against me. I moan when I feel him hard against my ass through his pants.

Why do I give in every time? What is it about this shifter's hold on me? I think about the way he guided me up and down on his dick and how I came all over him. I bite my lip and try to control my thoughts. I'm daydreaming so much that I don't realize it until Kane lifts me up and sits me on the kitchen counter.

He turns off the stove, pushes the pan away with his bare hand, and positions himself between my legs, gripping the back of my neck. He pulls me into a deep kiss. I'm no longer thinking about food or the phone. My hands go to his bare arms, savoring the smoothness of his skin, the firmness of his body.

I trace the contours of his muscles, feeling the hard lines beneath the softness of his chocolate skin. His biceps flex under my touch, solid and powerful.

I move my hands to his chest, feeling the rapid beat of his heart beneath the fabric of his tank top. Kane steps back, pulling his tank top over his head in one swift motion, revealing his broad, chiseled chest. I feel like I'm melting as I take in the sight of him, every ridge of his muscles high-lighted by the dim kitchen light.

"I can smell how wet you're getting," Kane says, his voice a low growl that makes my skin tingle.

He moves between my legs again, his hips pressing

against mine as he kisses me with a hunger that leaves me breathless. His tongue glides along my lips, begging for entrance, and I part them to let him in. He cups my chin, keeping my face steady as he devours me, his mouth claiming mine with a ferocity that makes my head spin.

"This is how you take care of me, Tami. Loving me. I don't need anything more from you." His words comfort me, and I whimper, spreading my legs wider for him.

Why does he keep saying and doing all the right things? It's like he's perfect, made just for me. I surrender to the cloud of lust between us, one that doesn't seem to be calming down. It's getting worse, more intense by the second. I feel this need to be under Kane all the time, and it doesn't help that he just gives in over and over.

When I moan against his lips and grind into him, he picks me up and carries me to the sofa, sitting down with me on top of him. "I know how much you like this position, baby," he says, pulling his member out of his pants. "You got so wet while you were riding me. Not a good position for making a baby, but it still feels great. What matters is your pleasure." I whimper at his words, thankful that he pulls down my panties this time, helping me stand so I can step out of them instead of ripping them off. Then I squat, and he guides me down onto his dick. I take in his full length, sliding right in.

"So wet, baby. You're so wet," he moans, his voice thick with desire. His hands grip my hips, guiding my movements as I ride him, lost in the sensation of him filling me completely.

It's like an addiction I can't control. Riding him, feeling the warmth of him stretching me out, and the way he fills me with his seed. I'm desperate to get pregnant.

I'm being so reckless right now. I feel my mind struggling with this, but my body belongs to him and my heart... I gasp when his hands start to lift me harder, faster, pushing me up and down on his dick. I'm soaking wet, my arousal coating my thighs as I feel my orgasm approaching.

I cling to his shoulders, nails digging into his skin as he thrusts up into me. His eyes are locked on mine, dark and intense, filled with a raw hunger that matches my own. I can't look away, even as the pleasure builds, higher and higher, until it's almost too much to bear.

"Kane," I moan, my voice trembling. "I'm so close."

"Let go, baby," he growls, his grip on my hips tightening. "I want to feel you come all over me."

That's all it takes. My body tenses, then shatters, waves of ecstasy crashing over me as I scream his name. Kane keeps going, driving into me, prolonging my pleasure until I'm a quivering, breathless mess in his arms.

With one final thrust, he comes with me, pushing so far into me that I can feel him in my gut as his seed spills into me. I come again from the sensation, my body seemingly needing every drop.

"Goddamn, just take it all, baby. Milk me. Take what you need from me." He pushes, and I scream, pulling myself against his chest and burying my face in his neck.

I feel this strange urge to bite him, to claim him and make him mine, so I bite down on his skin, but not hard enough to break it.

Kane moans and pushes himself into me even more. I whimper, pulling back and staring into his eyes, both of us breathing heavily. Kane gently brushes his hand against my cheek.

"You own me, Tami," he says, breathy. "You can take whatever you want from me, but you have to stay with me." His words make my heart flutter.

I bite down nervously on my lip, and a wave of sadness washes over me. Kane groans and pulls me against his chest. Still inside me, he stands, lifting me with him, and carries me up the stairs to the bathroom, gently pulling me out of him as he sets me down in the shower. He removes my nightdress while he takes off his sweatpants.

"Don't be afraid of this, baby," he says, stepping in with me, brushing a finger over my lip. He leans over me and starts the shower, pulling me close against him.

"It's just so hard to believe sometimes," I say, feeling the tears welling up in my eyes. "I've spent so much time alone, I thought..."

"Oh, Tami," he breathes, pulling me against his chest. I cling to him, digging my nails into his arms.

"I'm scared I'm going to lose you," I say in a shaky voice as I start to sob. "I don't want to lose you."

"It's never going to happen," he declares, then gently brushes his fingers over my claim mark. I relax immediately at the reminder that I belong to him. I pull back and look up at him, smiling.

"Let's get you cleaned up so you can make your phone calls." I nod and allow him to step out of the shower to grab some washcloths. He returns with soap and lathers the cloth, washing me from head to toe, making me feel like a princess.

AFTER OUR SHOWER, Kane helps me put on lotion and dress in another nightdress. This seems to be my usual attire when I'm with him. I don't mind; I feel relaxed, like all my troubles have gone away, even if only for a short while. He carries me back to the living room and sits me down in a chair at the bar, then he rounds the counter to finish breakfast.

"I want you to eat before you make your calls," he says. I smile and go along with it, my head deep in the clouds of love for him. He heats up the pancakes, scrambles some eggs, and serves me a plate, then sits beside me, gently rubbing my back as I eat.

He watches me for a while, then stands to get me a drink from the fridge. I gulp it down, then stand up. Watching him, I walk to the living room, grab my phone from the charger, and sit on the sofa, smiling when I hear Kane's grunts and groans again. He's so adorable.

I turn on my phone and immediately unlock it. The moment the screen lights up, I'm flooded with texts and voicemails, mostly from my job and Angie.

I start with my text messages, going through them one by one. I sigh when there's nothing from Tiffany. As I scroll, my eyes narrow at a message from an unknown number.

I glance at Kane, noticing he's cleaning up breakfast, then quickly open the text. My heart sinks—it's from Julian.

> Julian: Do you really think you can get away from me? I know where you are. You're mine, Tami.

Fear radiates through me. I quickly close the message, my fingers shaking, and immediately dial Angie's number for a FaceTime call. She answers on the second ring. The water immediately stops, and I know Kane smells a change in my scent.

"Tami!" Angie beams. She's not at work, and I'm glad. I don't want to explain over the phone in front of everyone why I left. Not that it matters; I just hate work gossip.

"I'm fine. I'm okay!" I tell her. She glares at me. Kane

comes into view, and Angie notices him. His green eyes are a dead giveaway.

"Holy shit, you really are in Wintermoon," she says, then looks away.

I try to stand from the sofa as soon as Kane sits down, but he grips my waist and pulls me into his lap. I squeal, and his smile widens, exposing his sharp canines. Angie gasps at the sight of them.

"So, you're mated to a shifter in Wintermoon, huh? Wow, how did that happen?" she mutters, and I can hear the sarcasm.

We'd talked about Wintermoon and how she wished she could relocate her children here. If she weren't mated to a shifter, she'd find a way to move. Yet here I am. I cringe at her comment, and Kane's face falls. I slide off his lap, glaring at him when he starts to grunt.

"It's a long story, Angie. I ran into trouble with Tiffany's boyfriend, Julian, and I had to take off for safety," I explain. I want to tell her something inside me told me to go to Wintermoon because of my connection with Kane, but I say nothing.

"Hmph," she says, then goes quiet. I can see she's not happy about me being here. "It's funny, you weren't interested in Wintermoon at all. You pushed it off like hope was far from you, yet here you are, in the lap of your shifter." She mutters, and I groan.

"I know, Angie. I..." I pause, at a loss for words. I look at Kane, who seems ready to snatch the phone from my hands. I shake my head and hold up my hand for him to wait. Angie chuckles, not believing this happened to me and not her. Damn, why is she turning on me like this?

"When I was running from Julian, I wanted to call you and maybe hide out at your place, but I paused. Something told me to keep driving north, that I would be safe. I can't explain it. I just knew I would be safe if I drove to Wintermoon. My car flipped and got totaled in the snowstorm, and Kane saved me."

"Why is it always the ones who don't even want this beautiful life who get it? This is so unfair!" Angie grumbles, and Kane growls.

I glare at him, realizing it was pointless to call. Angie sighs. "I guess it's back to the grind for me—living from check to check, trying to make it. If you're calling about your job, a lawyer already told us you were in Wintermoon, so we couldn't file a missing person's report. Julian showed up here twice looking for you. We told him where you were, so he'd back off." I gulp, and she ends the call. Kane snatches the phone from my hands, and it looks tiny in his palm.

"Julian is looking for you, huh?" he says with a sneer, and I see the darkness in his eyes. His wolf is coming out. Kane closes his palm, and the phone shatters in his hand. My eyes widen as I watch the tiny pieces crumple to the floor.

"I don't think you need a phone anymore, baby," he mutters, meeting my eyes.

Now I understand why there's a magical case for his tablet.

20

Kane

My wolf strains to burst out after hearing that Julian is looking for Tami. And Angie? Her voice was filled with nothing but jealousy and envy. She wasn't happy for Tami at all. Whether Tami noticed this, I don't know.

Frustration boils within me. Knowing that Julian is searching for my mate makes me want to hunt him down right now. I let the shattered pieces of her phone spill from my hand onto the floor as I watch Tami's eyes widen in fear.

"You broke my phone. Why?" She snaps at me.

"Anger," I answer simply, then stand, ready to go on a hunt. "I need to call on Kade. I'm going to look for Julian myself. I have his scent imprinted. It shouldn't be difficult to find him once I catch it."

Tami immediately stands from the sofa, shaking her head. I smile when her hand moves to her claim mark, her fingers brushing over the scar. She doesn't realize she's doing it. *The pull* has really taken hold of her, and I don't think she understands the changes happening in her body right now.

"No!" she shouts, making me pause. I need her to tell me. *The pull* is strong in her, but she still hasn't gotten the urge to claim me. Earlier, she was so close, so close, yet she still hesitated. She doesn't understand what's happening, so she won't know how to answer if I ask.

"Why not?" I ask, then start to move around her. She grabs my arm, trying to pull me back. I pause and look back at her.

"You go onto human territory and kill for me, that's not good. Let's wait and see what Kade finds," she insists, running a hand over her forehead.

Her scent keeps shifting from confusion to fear. That's a scent I normally smell when someone is hiding something. I glance down at her shattered phone, then back at her, narrowing my eyes. She saw something on it, and she's not as upset as I expected.

"Baby, you saw something on your phone. I can smell it on you." She gasps, backing away slowly.

I grin and follow her. Tami likes to hide things from me, thinking it's for my protection, but it's not. She doesn't need to protect me. I wish she'd stop trying.

I continue to stalk her, matching her steps backward. She eventually trips, hitting the end table, but I catch her, gripping her nightdress and pulling her back against my chest. She moans, frustrated, and puts her hand on my chest. I press my palm against her back, steadying her on her feet.

"First, I'm taking you to my village, then I'm going to hunt down the asshole looking for you," I tell her.

"No, please! I'll talk," she says quickly. I gesture toward

the sofa, and she nervously sits down. I go into the kitchen to grab a broom and dustpan to sweep up the mess.

"Start talking, Tami," I tell her. Her heartbeat quickens, but I also detect a hint of arousal. Damn, this woman really is turned on all the time.

I'm one lucky shifter.

She snaps her legs shut when she realizes where my eyes are going. There's no need for her to worry; I won't be using my dick this time. I'll use my tongue instead, something I know she'll enjoy.

"Julian texted me," she murmurs, avoiding my gaze. "But I couldn't make out what he said." A menacing growl escapes me, causing Tami to nervously jump off the sofa. She's lying; I can sense it in her scent.

"I need to talk to Kade," I mutter.

"Please don't leave me in your village alone," she begs.

Why not? My village is the safest place for her right now. Safer than here. I stand from the sofa and try to grab her, but she just runs off, trying to get away. My hand is on her waist before she can reach the stairs, pulling her back to me. She's so adorable, stubborn as she is. She kicks and fights me until we're back on the sofa with her plopped down on my lap.

"You're scaring me!" she yells, slapping at my chest.

I feel nothing but gentle caresses. Her feistiness is only making me hard, but now is not the time for that. I take my hand and gently press it against her throat, smoothing it over her claim mark. Her body goes limp immediately and she submits, her eyes rolling to the back of her head.

"What are you doing?" she mumbles incoherently.

"Calming you down," I tell her, moving my hand from her claim mark to her breasts.

Her arousal hits me like a tidal wave, and I think my dick

might burst through my sweatpants. She should be happy to see my village, meet my brothers and the sister mates.

Once her body relaxes, I grip the back of her neck and pull her into a sweet, loving kiss. She moans between my lips, but I keep the kiss brief, moving my hand to gently stroke her back while my other hand cups her ass.

"Oh," she breathes, looking into my eyes, dazed. "How? How did you do that?" I brush my fingers over her claim mark again.

"You're mine now, Tami. You'll submit to me even when you don't want to. You could hate me, but your body will always submit. I don't want my mate to hate me." I gently stroke her cheek. "I need you to tell me why you don't want me to leave you with my village." She answers quickly, and I smile, happy that my claim on her is working.

"Someone is always dropping me off somewhere and leaving me. I'm tired of it." Her eyes well with tears, and I can see the pain there. I sigh, hating that I made her feel this way. Tami is deep into this, and I suspect she'll claim me soon. I keep my thoughts calm before I speak again.

"I'm sorry, baby. I'm sorry for being so aggressive and scaring you. My wolf won't tolerate another man hunting you. I'm afraid I can't control that."

"You can't leave me," she demands, clutching my shirt. It's then I realize she doesn't need to claim me. Tami already owns me, and she owns my wolf too. I groan and lift her off my lap, gently placing her on the sofa.

I stand, looking down at her, and let out a frustrated sigh, then dash upstairs to our bedroom. I pull a shirt and a pair of thick leggings out of the drawer, along with some socks, then dart back down the stairs. She narrows her eyes at the clothes, wondering where I'm going with this.

"Get dressed. There's something I want to show you." I help her pull on the clothes.

When she's dressed, I walk to the door, grab her coat and boots, and drop to my knees to help her slide into them. She pulls her coat over her shoulders, and I help her button up. I open the front door and step outside, pulling her onto the porch with me. She looks at the dim sky for a moment, then back at me.

"Are we going to your workshop?" she asks, looking toward the shed. I shake my head.

"No, baby." I answer, then pull off my clothes. She puts her finger to her lips, going quiet.

"You're the only person who's ever tamed my wolf. And the way you just tamed me in the cabin tells me you can handle him. You're going to ride my wolf and let him take you through the forest. Can you do that for me?" She nods eagerly, an adorable smile on her lips.

I leap from the porch, shifting mid-air. Its paws land on the snow, the cold invigorating. My wolf turns and growls softly, then drops to a sitting position in front of the porch. Tami looks around nervously for a moment, then slowly steps down. My wolf lowers himself to the snow.

"Hi, Kane's wolf," she says warmly. "Kane said you are going to take me through the forest." She brushes her fingertips against my wolf's snout, and my wolf closes his eyes, a low moan escaping.

Tami owns my wolf. She walks around me, gripping his fur, and climbs on top. Once she's settled, my wolf stands, feeling her grip tighten.

My wolf moves slowly at first, turning away from the cabin and heading toward the forest, making sure she's comfortable. He looks back at Tami, and our eyes meet. She smiles and gives a nervous nod.

"I'm ready... Well, I think," she says. My wolf barks in response and takes off into the forest.

The air rushes past us as my wolf maneuvers through the trees, its paws barely making a sound on the ground. Tami holds on tightly, but there's no fear in her eyes—just excitement and joy. The cold wind bites at us, but it's refreshing. I can feel her laughter vibrating through my wolf's fur, and it fills me with happiness.

We jump over fallen logs and weave through the dense forest. The moonlight illuminates the path. The forest is alive with sounds, but all I can focus on is the feeling of Tami on my wolf's back, trusting me completely.

After what seems like forever and yet only a moment, he brings us to a smooth stop. My wolf's paws slide slightly as we leap from a small hill, landing perfectly with Tami. We arrive at the edge of the waters where the lakes connect, overlooking lower Michigan and Mackinac Island.

My wolf sits down, and Tami climbs off, taking in the view with wide eyes. The sight before us is breathtaking.

The icy lake glistens under the dim daylight, and the distant lights of Mackinac Island twinkle like stars. Tami's breath catches, and she turns to me, her eyes full of wonder.

"It's beautiful," she whispers, awed.

I shift back into human form, sitting naked on the cool ground, which doesn't affect me. Tami starts to pull off her coat, but I stop her.

"I'm fine, baby. I just wanted you to see this." Tami looks around, still amazed.

Nightfall will be here soon, as winter days are shorter. I reach out for her, but her eyes are focused on the scenery. We can't stay here long; the cool temperatures will be too much for her. I can simply shift into my wolf form to keep warm. I stretch my arm to grip her coat, pulling her into my lap.

"You did so well, letting my wolf carry you." She wraps her arms around my neck and snuggles against me.

"That's it! You win the best first date award!" she jokes. I chuckle in response. First date? How do I tell her that now that I've claimed her, we are practically married? I bite my tongue, holding back that comment. We are having a beautiful moment. I don't want to scare her.

"It was fun, like riding a rollercoaster. I knew I was safe with your wolf. He was so careful with me the entire ride."

"My wolf loves..." I pause, clearing my throat. She pulls back and stares into my eyes with a bright smile.

"Go on," she taunts. I shift her focus to the lake.

"Look," I say, pointing at the small cruise ship heading our way. I wasn't expecting more tourists; I was hoping for a quiet moment. Tami tries to stand, but I pull her back into my lap.

"Unless you want everyone to see me in my birthday suit," I joke, and she quickly nods, understanding, but wiggles her ass against me to taunt me.

Does she not think I won't take her right here in this weather? My body heat would keep her warm. But she rests her back against my chest while I keep my arms wrapped around her.

"I used to dream of coming here. I even used to buy lottery tickets before I gave up," she murmurs, staring at the ship. It's a cruise liner that sails from Detroit to Mackinac Island multiple times a day, but it only docks in Detroit.

"Why did you give up, baby?" I ask, curious.

"It felt like a fairytale. Like I was hoping for something that was so far out of reach." I smile and shake my head.

"It was closer than you knew."

"What was your life like after the curse? Did you have a girlfriend? Did you love her?" she asks, and I laugh at the question.

"I slept with women sometimes, yes. But I could never love. I could never make a baby either. You are the only woman who can provide that to me." I say, moving my hand first to her heart, then slowly down to her belly, pressing my palm against it. I've bred her well enough for my seed to take root in her. I hope it does. Tami surprises me, placing her hand over mine, giving me hope that she feels the same.

"I don't need any of my old stuff from my apartment. Tell Kade to throw it out. I want to start new memories with you." Her words make my heart pound, and my hand tightens against her.

"You're lucky we have an audience, baby," I tease, and she giggles.

21

Tami

The cruise ship passes, and I turn my face away from the flashing lights and the tourists' yells. The ship is enormous, with three levels, and it appears to be at full capacity. The captain honks the horn, and Kane waves as I pull back. He gently runs his fingers through my curls, soothing me.

"I get why you don't like the attention," he says softly. "I hate it too."

Once the ship passes, I pull my head from his chest. He continues to stroke my hair as I look back out at the water. His body feels warm against mine. I notice an island next to Mackinac Island and wonder what it's used for.

"The other island, what's it for?" I ask.

"King Amir lives there. He's the first vampire and ruler of all supernaturals," he answers.

"The first vampire?" I repeat, turning back to him.

He smiles and nods. "House of Zorah has a strong bond with King Amir. We served him in the Great War and during many of his travels before the curse. My family are great carpenters and architects. My brothers Levi, Micah, and Gabriel are building the new palace. I'll take you there one day to meet our King."

He plants a gentle kiss on my forehead, then lifts me from his lap and stands, looking over the waters, completely naked.

"I brought you here because this is where I used to come and pray to Fate for you. Asking, begging her to bring you to me," he says, looking back at me. "Years went by, and I'd switch up patrolling with my brothers until Levi and Micah found their mates. It was hard for me, watching them find happiness while I had none. I told Kade I'd take on patrolling full-time. I wanted you so badly, Tami. Just to fulfill my duty to you."

I start to stand, but Kane walks over to me, kneeling to help me up.

"I'm so happy, Tami. I finally have you. But eventually, I'm going to have to share you. And I'm struggling with that," he admits.

I squeeze his hand and look out at the waters. This place is so beautiful and serene. I could stay here all day.

"It's getting dark. Let me shift back into my wolf so I can take you home," he tells me.

"Can we come back here again?" I ask.

Kane steals a tender, loving kiss from me before he steps back. "Yes, baby. I'll bring you back here again."

He shifts into his wolf form, massive and imposing with sharp emerald, green eyes, thick black fur, big paws with sharp claws, and monstrous teeth.

His wolf walks over to me and gently brushes his snout against my cheek. I smile and embrace him, cupping his face with both hands and planting a gentle kiss on his snout. The wolf whimpers, then sticks out his long tongue, swiping it against my cheek. I giggle and smile at him with pride.

"I love you too, Kane's wolf," I say with a bright smile, running my hands through his fur.

His wolf stiffens and backs away, but I notice its tail wagging. I can see it in his eyes. Kane's wolf is happy. I put a finger to my lips as if it's supposed to be a secret.

"Don't tell Kane," I tease.

His wolf sits down and stares at the water quietly for a moment. I wonder if he's praying to Fate again. I keep quiet and watch until he turns back to me, then lowers his body for me to climb on.

"Can I give you a name? I hate calling you Kane's wolf," I ask. He huffs in response. He doesn't want to be named. I shrug and climb onto his back, gripping a handful of his fur.

Once he's sure I'm secure, he stands and takes slow steps away from the border, carrying me back into the forest. He jumps the hill and breaks into a run.

The thrill of the run ignites something in me. The way his wolf moves through the snowy forest with ease but is also careful so that I don't fall or lose my balance.

It's like something out of a dream. In minutes, we arrive back at the cabin. He immediately slows and lowers himself when he reaches the porch steps. I climb off him with a groan, but I don't want to let him go. His wolf starts to stand, but I hold up my hand, stopping him.

"Wait," I say, and he pauses immediately, sitting down. I go over to the porch steps and sit down, staring at him.

"Let me just stay with you for a while. I like Kane and all, but you are my favorite part of him," I say with a smile. We stay put until I start to shiver from the cold air.

That makes Kane's wolf stand up and back away. Night

has fallen, and I look up at the beautiful dim sky, wondering how I got so lucky. I close my eyes and silently thank Fate.

Kane's wolf shifts back into human form. I smile when I feel his fingers brush against my cheek and open my eyes.

"Hey," I murmur. He scoops me into his arms, cradling me against his chest as he climbs the porch steps and carries me back into the cabin.

Kane is quiet as he sets me down and helps me out of my boots and coat. He walks me to the sofa to sit me down, then goes to the fireplace and lights a fire.

"I'm going to put on some clothes, then come back down and cook you dinner. Stay here and relax," he says, then leans down, his face inches from mine.

"My wolf..." he murmurs, his nose brushing against mine, "I can hear you through my wolf." He presses his lips against mine tenderly. I gasp and swallow when he pulls back. His eyes linger on me for a moment, then he smiles and walks off.

I stand nervously from the sofa and start to pull off my leggings and shirt, leaving me in my nightdress. I grab a blanket and make myself comfortable on the sofa.

This is the happiest I've ever been in my life. But I'm not used to keeping anything.

After seeing the beautiful view of the lakes from Wintermoon, I want to see more. I'm ready to go into the village and meet Kane's pack. And I'd like to help out around the village if I can. I'm sure my skills as a CNA will be useful here. I think back to the moments at the border and cringe. Kane said he could hear me through his wolf.

That means he heard me when I said I loved him. I hear his heavy footsteps in the bedroom, traveling into the hallway, then down the stairs. I don't look over the sofa to see him.

The steps go quiet, and I lift my head to look around, surprised that he's not at the stairs or in the kitchen. Where did he go? I gasp when I turn my head, only to find his face inches from mine again. My head jerks back and he smiles, moving closer to me.

"How did you?" I ask, still processing how he was so quiet.

"I could tell you were listening for me. When I hunt, I can quiet my movements so that my prey doesn't notice I'm stalking them." He gently kisses my forehead. "What would you like to eat for dinner?"

"Were you just hunting me?" I ask him. He chuckles and brushes his fingers over my claim mark. I close my eyes from his touch, my body going limp. How does he do that?

"Tell me what to feed you, baby," he says. I feel dazed and confused, but eager to answer him.

"I don't know, chicken or tuna," I tell him. He smiles and stands upright, pulling his hand away from me.

"I've already made you chicken," he says, pondering. "I'll go with tuna." Then he walks away, his heavy footsteps returning to normal. I sink into the sofa, still feeling strange from his touch. I'm getting comfortable here, with Kane. I'm not used to having something to hold onto.

I pray that I get to keep him forever.

22

Kane

Six Weeks Later

Watching Tami sleep is the highlight of my mornings. The way her chest rises and falls, the way her body sinks into the mattress— she's truly comfortable with me right now. She's content.

I need to gather a list of supplies. We've been shacked up in this cabin for over a month, both of us lost in this perfect moment between us. I'm pushing it, trying to stretch our supplies as much as possible, but it's time to stock up again.

Now, I'm faced with the decision to take Tami to my village. I'm not looking forward to it. I keep thinking about how she'll be away from me all day, spending time with the mated sisters, while I work on my carpentry projects.

Tami moans and shifts on the bed, turning her back towards me. She's a wild sleeper and tends to mumble in her sleep. I don't mind it. I'll take Tami however she comes. She's my mate, my forever.

I'll never complain about something so trivial when I've spent a thousand years alone. I roll onto my back, deep in thought. It's difficult being just inches away from her for too long.

Even when I considered taking Tami to my village while I hunted Julian, my intention was never for her to stay there. I planned to bring her back to this cabin.

Yet, I don't consider this cabin home. These feelings about Tami confuse me. I don't want to share her, yet I don't want to keep her isolated. Tami deserves to meet other supernaturals in Wintermoon.

I let out a frustrated sigh, knowing what I must do, yet my thoughts are pulling me in different directions. Suddenly, I wrinkle my nose at the shift in Tami's scent. It's gone from sweet country apples to something woody and musky.

I don't like it. My hand reaches out to grab her, almost rough, when I detect someone else's scent on her. But I pull back and try to calm myself. The last thing I want is to hurt her. I need to think rationally. No one has been near her in a month. It's only been me. So, either there's been a change in my scent, or she's pregnant.

My eyes widen at the theory.

Tami is pregnant. My woman is going to give me a pup.

My wolf howls inside me, overjoyed by this news, and my entire body stiffens. I need to confirm this. I know how it works. There will be a change in her scent, she'll taste different, and I'll start to hear our pup's heartbeat. I need to lick her right now.

Tami rolls onto her back, cute little snores and huffs escaping her lips. The change in her scent just happened.

It's going to take time for her body to recognize the pregnancy, and she'll start to experience changes.

I remember the days when my pack was full of life. As a young pup, I watched my father coach newly mated males on pregnancy and how important it was not to tell our women before they figured it out themselves.

It was agonizing for newly mated men to hold back. Now, here I am, in the same position. I'm desperate to tell her. I want to shift into my wolf and howl at the moon, thanking Fate for this gift. It's all I ever wanted.

A wave of emotions hits me, and I start to sob, tears welling in my eyes. Finally, I have my mate, and now, a pup. I know I should let her sleep, but I need her.

I slowly climb on top of Tami, careful not to put my weight on her. She's in a deep sleep, her breathing slow and even. I take in her scent, a mix of musk and wood. I inhale deeply and smile, loving the scent of our baby.

I lean down and plant a gentle kiss on her cheek. She moans and tries to turn to her side but is blocked by my arm. She rolls back with a sigh, giving up.

I lean into her, sniffing her scent, finally catching a whiff of the country apple fragrance I've imprinted to remember forever. She turns her head to the side, revealing her claim mark.

Moving my head down her body, I continue taking in her scent until I'm positioned between her legs. I gently lift her legs and spread them wide, then pull up her nightdress, exposing her pink silk panties.

The musky scent is potent, mixed with her own scent. She is very much pregnant. Curling my fingers around the fabric, I slide her panties aside, revealing her glistening sex.

The smell brings my arousal to life. I'm aching to be inside her, but a taste will be more than enough. I also need to get our baby's room ready and make our home comfortable for Tami. She'll need a place to start nesting.

I swipe my tongue gently against her folds, and her body reacts immediately. She moans and gently bucks her hips towards me, craving more.

"Kane," she moans, and the sound of my name only turns me on more.

Her hands search for me until they reach the back of my head, pushing me into her. I brush my tongue up and down her folds, swirling it around her clit before dragging my tongue down and thrusting it inside her.

Tami's legs start to kick, her body trying to push away, but I grip her thighs and pull her back, pushing my tongue as far as it will go. She screams and sits up, her eyes snapping open as she watches me lick her, pushing her to orgasm. Her legs start to shake, and she gives in to the pleasure.

Her orgasm slams into her, and she jerks, trying to pull away, her toes curling as she climaxes. I keep going, thrusting my tongue in and out of her, swirling around the walls of her sex, taking the cream she produces. I can taste the change in her flavor, the mix of country apples and woody essence. I moan and push my face into her again.

"Kane!" Tami shouts, her body going limp on the bed.

I pout and pull away reluctantly. I'd stay between her legs all day, but I know that's not possible.

I need to get supplies for her. Stretching what we have isn't an option, especially now that she's pregnant. Should I stop being selfish and just take her with me? That would mean introducing her to my pack.

I can't keep her stuck here in the cabin. She'll need the company of her sister mates and medical care. Every pregnant mate must attend monthly prenatal care at the Wintermoon hospital, a facility created by Kade and Leah, along with my brothers who were architects for most of Wintermoon's development.

Kissing her thighs, I look up to see her smiling, staring up at the ceiling.

"Is it always going to be like this?" she breathes out, not looking at me. "I'll never want to leave if it is." I release her leg and place my head on her abdomen. As long as I'm close enough this early in the pregnancy, I'll hear our baby's heartbeat. Tami moans and runs her fingers through my hair as I listen.

"What are you doing?" she asks, laughing softly. I don't answer her. I drown out all the sounds around us, focusing on the one sound I'm looking for.

The soft, rapid thud of our baby's heartbeat swooshes in my ears. It's the most beautiful sound I've ever heard. I close my eyes and let out a relieved sigh, so happy to have this moment. It's such a strong heartbeat. Our pup is strong.

"Oh my god, Kane!" Tami shouts when she feels my hand slide between her legs. She is in for a long morning of orgasms.

23

Tami

"What do you mean I can't go into Wintermoon with you for shopping?" I grumble, pacing the floor of our bedroom.

Kane's acting weird. I'm in the biggest mood funk I've been in in a long time. What the hell is going on with me? I smooth my hand over my belly, wondering if it's PMS. Kane just sits at the edge of the bed, watching me.

I don't understand why he won't let me go. He had no problem with the idea of leaving me in his village to chase after Julian several weeks ago.

Now, he just wants me to sit here and wait for him to come back. I don't want to stay cooped up in this cabin. I'd like to get out, breathe some fresh air, and see the sunshine. I want to socialize and meet the other mates of Wintermoon.

"Just trust me on this, baby. You don't need to be out walking around town right now," he says, and I glare at him.

"You're just ashamed to be seen in public with me!" I snap, pulling at my curls.

Kane's eyes narrow, and he stands from the bed. He can probably smell my mood shift. I feel insecure, and I don't want to talk about it.

"What are you talking about, baby?" he says. He starts to move my way, but I turn away from him and dart out of the room, heading downstairs.

He follows me, and in this one-bedroom cabin, there isn't anywhere to hide from him.

I try to busy myself in the fridge, but it's nearly empty. Barely any juice or milk. I close the fridge and go into the back room, where we keep most of our bulk pantry items and the deep freezer. It's nearly empty too.

I open the deep freezer, scowling at the few packages of meat inside. I'm hungry, and my options are very limited! He has to go into town; I can't stop him, or we'll be left with his hunts as my food source. I rub my belly again, scratching my head. I'm so irritated right now, and my breasts are sore.

Kane must have squeezed them too hard during sex this morning. As soon as I step out of the back room, I yelp when Kane grips my waist, lifting me off the floor, and carries me back to the kitchen. He sets me down on the counter, caging me in with his hands on either side of me.

"Ashamed of you, Tami? Where did that come from?" I shrug at him.

Because I don't know honestly. But it's the only conclusion I can come up with. He doesn't want me with him, and it's bothering me.

I don't answer him, shaking my head away when he tries to cup my face. A wave of emotions hits me, and tears well up in my eyes. Kane roughly cups my face, forcing me to meet his gaze.

"Dammit, Tami!" he growls, but I can't stop. It hurts that

he doesn't want me with him. He sighs and presses his forehead to mine.

"It's not that I don't want you with me, baby. I do. I want you with me now more than anything. But it's not safe for you to travel right now," he tells me, then plants a gentle kiss on my forehead. I don't understand why he keeps saying that.

Not safe? Did Julian find me and he's trying to keep me safe? A shudder of fear ripples through me, and I shake nervously. He turns away from me and goes to the fridge, grabbing the last jar of milk.

"We've got some pancake mix and a pack of bacon. I'll cook all of it, so you have something to munch on while I'm gone." He pours me a glass and hands it to me. I take a sip, instantly tasting something sour, and spit it out in the sink.

Kane steps back, wondering what's wrong, but he doesn't say anything. I pull the cup to my nose and sniff. It doesn't smell off. I try to take another sip, only to spit it out again.

"I can't drink this! Water, shifters only drink water!" I blurt out, then pour the milk out and set the glass in the sink, wiping my mouth.

I pause, realizing what I just said. Why did I say that? I look up at Kane, who's got the biggest smile on his face. I want to slap it off. I try to jump down from the counter, but he catches me, gripping my waist and placing me back on the counter.

"I'll get you some water, baby," he says, then grabs a clean glass and fills it with ice, then runs the tap water. The moment he hands it to me, I gulp it down as if I'm dying of thirst. He smiles and takes the glass, pouring me another.

I run a hand over my belly again, getting my thoughts together. That outburst, coupled with the sore breasts and mood swings, and Kane's odd behavior... Then I think back to the last time I had a period.

"I'm pregnant," I murmur. Kane sets the glass down and moves between my legs.

"Finally!" he says in an exasperated tone, then cups my face and pulls me into a tender kiss.

Oh my god, I'm pregnant. I don't know why I'm so surprised. I've been with him constantly. He's an addiction, that's what he is to me. I can't get enough of this man.

And his sweetness, the way he takes care of me. No one has ever... I start to sob, feeling an overwhelming wave of emotions. My hand goes to my belly, pressing my palm against it.

"You knew already?" I ask.

"I noticed a change in your scent this morning. When I rested my head on your belly, I heard the heartbeat. It's faint because it's early in the pregnancy, but it's strong." I place a hand on his cheek, feeling overwhelmed.

He notices and immediately scoops me into his arms and carries me to the sofa, sitting down with me in his lap. I wrap my arms around him, holding him close. I'm so happy I can't find the words.

"This is why you don't want me to come shopping with you? Because I'm pregnant?"

"Yes and no," he answers. I pull back and look into his eyes.

"I need to take you back to the village so you can start getting to know the pack. But that means I have to share you. My cabin isn't ready for you. I don't want to lose the closeness we have right now. Can't I just keep you to myself for a little longer?" I smile and let out a sigh of relief. Kane's just being clingy. I don't mind, but seclusion is no way to raise our baby.

"Promise me we'll go to the village in another month or two? I don't want to have this baby alone. And I need to see a doctor. Are there doctors for shifter parents?" He laughs and gently strokes my back.

"Yes, we have medical centers. You'll be paired with a midwife. When we finally get to the village, the sister mates will stay close to you until you have the baby. Meanwhile, I'll spend my time preparing our home. I'll carve all the furniture and help you decorate."

"This is happening so fast, but I want this. I really do. I'm happy, Kane," I tell him. He smiles and pulls me into a loving kiss.

"I won't be long. We need supplies badly. I was able to go over a month because I hunt for my food. But I can't put this trip off any longer. I need to go, baby. And I want you to stay here and wait for me. You're safe in Wintermoon. No one is stupid enough to try and take you from me," he says, and I can see it in his eyes. He'll kill anyone who tries. I smile and nod. He sighs, as if it's painful for him to do this, but he lifts me off his lap, gently placing me on the sofa and stands.

"I'll make the pancakes, then I'll go. I'll only be gone a few hours, and I want my woman and baby resting." I put my feet up on the sofa and give him a mock salute. He laughs and heads into the kitchen. I place my hands over my belly, still coming to terms with the fact that I'm going to be a mom.

24

Tami

Kane's been gone for hours, half the day, and I'm starting to worry. There's no way for me to call him. When he left, he just took the trailer and went on his way. Kane doesn't drive. He can, but he prefers walking or running, so it takes him longer to get places.

The sun starts to set, and I'm fully dressed, ready to go out and help him unload the trailer. I know he'll be upset about it, but I don't care. I miss him and I've been away from him all day. *The pull* is getting stronger, and I don't like it. It's agonizing how much I miss him right now. I hear the trees rustling and heavy footsteps crunching through the snow.

I immediately spring into action, running to the door and sliding on my boots, grabbing my scarf and coat. I throw open the door and race down the porch steps, careful not to slip. I look around, sniffing the air as if I can find him that way. I've been acting weird all day.

Kane was right, the pregnancy has started to change me. I can only drink water. I tried some leftover juice and couldn't keep it down. Our baby only wants water. I could barely stomach the bacon and pancakes, but I ate them anyway.

Darkness quickly falls as I stand outside, waiting for him to come into view. Our cabin has a small road that leads to the main one, which takes you into Wintermoon. No one ever comes here except for the small shipping truck to collect Kane's furniture for sale on the island.

The trees rustle again, sending a gust of cold wind in my direction. I shiver, clutching my coat tighter. Maybe I should zip it up. A shadow appears on the small hilltop that leads to the main road, and I gasp. It's not Kane.

His dark ebony skin stands out against the white snowflakes clinging to his broad shoulders. His striking silver eyes almost seem to glow. A thick, well-groomed beard frames his full lips, which hint at a mysterious smile.

His tightly wound dreadlocks are dusted with snow, giving him a unique look. Pulled back slightly, they reveal a strong jawline and high cheekbones. He's wearing only a t-shirt and sweatpants, his bare feet buried in the snow. With his hands by his sides, he walks down the small slope toward me.

I'm unsure whether to run back inside the cabin or stay and talk to this imposing man. Something about him makes me stay put, almost as if I'm drawn to him. His steps are slow and careful, as if he's trying to keep me comfortable. I remain still as he approaches and comes into full view. He stops just a few feet away, practically towering over me.

He slowly leans in, then takes a sharp breath. I wince but remain still because I don't know this man. But there's a familiarity to him; he reminds me of Kane in a way. Is this one of his brothers?

"Tamera," he says in a low, husky voice, then starts to

circle around me as if he's sizing me up. "But you like to be called Tami, correct?" My head turns, following his movements as he circles me.

"Who are you?" I ask, but it comes out more like a demand. He smiles, flashing his white teeth. His canines are long and sharp, just like Kane's.

"I'm Levi, alpha of House of Zorah, and Kane's brother," he announces. I gasp, looking away from him.

"Oh," I blurt out, unsure how to address the alpha of the pack, so I let my head fall, not meeting his eyes. He stops in front of me, his hand coming to my chin, lifting it to meet his gaze. His silver eyes are stunning but also terrifying.

"The women don't bow to the men in my pack. We've waited centuries for you. You will be worshipped, not driven to be some house slave to make a man's life easier." I swallow and nod nervously as he removes his finger from my chin. He leans in again, taking a big whiff of my scent, then his hand immediately presses against my abdomen.

"You're pregnant." He murmurs. I step back from his hand, not wanting him to touch me.

"Kane went to the village to get supplies. He's not here."

"Not yet." He says with a sneer.

"I—I'm going inside until he gets back," I tell him. He gestures toward the cabin.

"Good, you shouldn't be out in the cold like this. And you certainly shouldn't be here all alone. I know what Kane is up to. I'm putting a stop to this tonight." He mutters, folding his arms over his chest. I start to turn and walk away but pause when I hear that comment. Wait, what? Stop what tonight?

I should go inside for safety, but the stubborn part of me won't let this go. I storm over to him and point my finger at his chest. He smiles, which makes me even more nervous.

"You don't know me, but I know Kane. Whatever you're about to do, just stop." I tell him.

"You are going to provide strong pups to my pack. You're very strong-willed." He smiles again and takes a step back, giving me a wink, "Incoming." I let my hand drop to my side and look around. The trees are rustling again, more intensely than Levi's arrival.

"Kane's not happy that I'm here," Levi says with a smile. I look around for any sight of him, gasping when something leaps out of the trees.

It's Kane. His large frame flies through the air and lands between me and Levi, the impact nearly knocking me off my feet. I start to fall back, but Kane catches me by my coat, pulling me back to my feet, holding me until I'm steady. His eyes never leave Levi's.

"You could have brought her home, brother. Keeping her shacked up here in this cabin and pregnant..." Levi growls, shaking his head, "this is unacceptable."

"I have a right to be alone with my mate for as long as I need. You have no right to question me about my decisions with my family." Kane snaps back. He releases me and gets into his brother's face. Both of them are massive, but Levi is larger. Levi smiles and remains unmoved by Kane's stance.

"I just discovered her pregnancy this morning. My plan was to bring her back to the village." Kane argues, but Levi just laughs.

"I heard whispers from Wintermoon. They say you brought a trailer filled with months' worth of supplies. Were you planning on bringing Tami into the village before or after the baby was born?" Kane doesn't answer him.

"This ends tonight. I want you and your mate in our village before sunrise. That's an order." Levi says, then starts to turn away.

"No." Kane's answer is simple and final. Levi turns around, looking almost stunned, as if he can't believe he's being challenged.

I flinch when a cloud of black smoke appears out of nowhere, sparkling with gold. My mouth drops open in shock as Kade appears from the smoke, wearing her sheriff's uniform. Her blue eyes and vampire smile dazzling. She looks at me, beaming that smile, and I'm not sure whether to blush or be terrified. How did she do that? Then I remember, she's a hybrid vampire-witch.

"Looks like I'm just in time for the dog fight," she beams. I glare at her. That comment is not helpful. Levi and Kane look at her for a moment, then go back to fight mode. She's supposed to be the sheriff of Wintermoon. Why isn't she breaking this up?

"No? Did I hear that correctly?" Levi moves closer to Kane.

"You did."

I look at Kade, and her eyes widen, a smile crossing her face. Oh my god, she's enjoying this.

"Will you do something!" I snap at her. She looks at me with a pout, then sighs.

"Fine!" She gives an exasperated shrug.

"Levi, back down. Kane just found his mate, and he needs to..." Levi holds up his hand, clearly irritated.

"Stand down? I think you forget who you're talking to." Levi sneers. Kane growls and steps back but doesn't defend Kade.

"I'm sheriff of Wintermoon, and you took an oath when you first arrived here." Kade reminds him.

"To the Master Coven, Kade. You are just the sheriff of Wintermoon. You don't have authority over me and how I rule over my pack. This is pack business and none of yours."

He growls. He moves closer to Kade, but she remains unfazed.

"I remember when he turned you. A traitorous witch against her own coven because you didn't agree with their summoning demons during the Great War. I carried your nearly dead body to King Amir at his request. House of Zorah has constructed some of the most historical palaces that still stand today. You are a youngling. They may call you *Mother Kade* here, but you are just Kade, the youngling, to me. I may as well be your uncle. Stay out of pack business!" Levi growls.

Shit.

Levi is something. Kade still stands unfazed, but I can see the irritation in her eyes. Levi moves back to Kane, getting right in his face.

"Agree to return to our village tonight, or I'll make you submit in front of your mate." Levi warns. Kane smiles, keeping his hands at his side.

"I told you, Levi. When I'm ready." Kane snaps back. Levi laughs and starts to back away. I try to move towards Kane, but he holds up his hand. Almost immediately, Kade grabs my arm and pulls me back. I try to snatch my arm away, but she has an iron grip.

"Let go of me." I snap. She ignores me, pulling me up the stairs to the porch.

"No, the alpha has given an order, and Kane needs to be tamed. You'll stand back until they're finished," she says. I gape at her. Kane and Levi start to strip down. I look away because I don't want to see them naked.

"Why are you letting this happen?" I ask her. She shrugs, never taking her eyes off them.

"This is pack business, Tami. And honestly, Kane shouldn't be keeping you here. You're a daughter of Wintermoon now, and he's keeping you cooped up in this cabin. Isn't that what you were running from in the beginning?" I fall silent. I've been in such a love haze, intoxicated by Kane, that I didn't even notice. Kade places her hand on my belly and smiles.

"You're giving Wintermoon a new baby. You deserve so much more than this, and Kane knows that. He's just being selfish, not wanting to share you."

"What's about to happen?" I ask, and Kade smiles.

"Time for that dog fight. This might push you to finally claim your mate."

25

Tami

A push? What push? I watch as Kane and Levi stand naked and shift into their wolf forms.

Levi's wolf form is almost the same as Kane's but larger. He's massive, with a thick coat of black fur and glowing silver eyes. He takes slow steps toward Kane's wolf. Kane's wolf growls, muscles tense, clearly fighting against Levi's dominance.

Levi's wolf gets closer, a deep growl rumbling in his chest. Kane's wolf lowers his head slightly, as if submitting, but he's struggling with it. I know Kane's wolf is wild and untamed, but he's submitted to me before. I don't like this one bit. I try to step forward to stop them, but Kade gently pushes me back.

"Tami, stop. I'm not letting you put yourself in danger," Kade says, causing me to groan. I huff and push her hands away.

Kane's wolf continues to struggle. He growls and barks at Levi's wolf, who steps closer, his size forcing Kane's wolf to lower his head further. Just when I think it's over and Kane's wolf has submitted, he lunges at Levi, and a wolf fight breaks out.

The two wolves clash in front of the cabin, their snarls tearing through the cold night. Snow flies in all directions as their massive bodies collide. Levi's wolf, larger and more powerful, uses his weight to pin Kane's wolf down, but Kane's wolf wriggles free, snapping his jaws at Levi's throat.

Kane's wolf circles, his eyes locked on Levi's, searching for an opening. Levi's wolf growls deeply and lunges again, forcing Kane's wolf to dodge and counter. They move in a flurry of fur and fangs, each trying to gain the upper hand.

Kane's wolf manages to grip Levi's shoulder, shaking his head violently. Levi's wolf howls in pain but quickly retaliates, swiping a massive paw across Kane's face. Blood splatters against the snow, stark red against white.

Kane's wolf falters, momentarily disoriented. Levi's wolf seizes the opportunity, barreling into Kane's side and knocking him off his feet. Kane's wolf scrambles to rise, but Levi's wolf is relentless, pressing his advantage and pinning Kane's wolf down by the throat.

Kane's wolf thrashes, trying to break free, but Levi's grip doesn't budge. Slowly, the fight drains out of Kane's wolf. His growls turn to whimpers, his body going limp in submission. Levi's wolf holds him there for a moment longer, ensuring his dominance is clear.

Finally, Levi's wolf releases Kane's throat and steps back, his silver eyes still intense. Kane's wolf lies in the snow, breathing heavily, his head lowered in defeat.

I stand there, heart pounding, feeling a mix of fear and helplessness. The fight is over, and Kane's wolf has lost.

Kade looks at me with a smile. "See, that wasn't so bad, now, was it?" Levi and Kane shift back into human form, their bodies covered in blood. I run down the stairs and into Kane's arms. He holds me, then bows before Levi.

"I understand now, Alpha. We'll return to the village in the morning." Levi looks at Kade with a growl as he slips into his pants, then takes off running into the forest.

"It's okay, Tami," Kane assures me, though it doesn't feel okay with him covered in blood.

"Kade, why are you here?" Kane asks as he grabs his clothes from the snowy ground. He heads back toward the cabin. Why is he acting like this was nothing?

"I'll wait here," Kade says. "I need to talk to you about something." Kane growls at her, but she laughs and stays outside while he leads me inside, slamming the door behind us.

Kane tosses his clothes to the floor and gently cups my face. "I'm sorry you had to see that, baby. But wolves... I need to take a shower." He turns away, heading upstairs. I follow him, tears streaming down my face. I could have lost him. It looked like Levi was about to take him from me. When we reach the bedroom, Kane stops me at the doorway.

"Go relax, baby. I'll be down in a minute. I just need to wash the blood off." He turns away, but I follow, pulling off my clothes and still crying. Kane groans and starts the shower.

"Tami..."

"Shut up! I thought I was going to lose you! You're acting like it was some playful tussle. You're covered in blood!" I scream, sobbing uncontrollably.

I strip naked and step into the shower, folding my arms over my chest. Kane sighs and climbs in with me. He stands under the shower head, the hot water running over his body.

I stare in awe as I watch his wounds heal before my eyes,

the water washing the blood away. I place my hand on his chest, my fingers brushing over one of the cuts as it closes up immediately.

"See, I'm okay, baby. It was just a disagreement between brothers." He cups my face and leans down, kissing me gently.

It doesn't make me feel any better. It may have been just a minor disagreement for him, but to me, it was a potential loss. The ache in my chest is unbearable.

I don't know how to be a mother, let alone to a shifter baby. I need him now more than ever. I feel an urge to bite down on his neck. I step back, and his eyes narrow, wondering what I'm doing. I can't control my urges or understand why this is happening.

"Tami," he breathes out, reaching for me. I shake my head, trying to back away, not understanding what's happening.

"I don't know what's wrong with me," I say. He moves closer, and the urge to claim him grows even stronger.

"Baby," he says, gripping my arm.

I try to pull away, not wanting to bite him, but I can't fight the urge. I leap into his arms, wrapping my legs around him, and bite down hard on his neck. Blood pools in my mouth as he falls back against the shower wall, struggling to stand. I moan, taking as much of his blood as I can. He steadies himself and gently rubs my back instead of pushing me away.

"That's right, baby, take what you need. I'm yours. I'm yours." He murmurs. He's encouraging me to drink more, and I do, gnawing at his flesh, taking as much blood as I want.

"We're one now, baby. Keep drinking. Claim me." He pushes, then takes his shaft and positions it at my entrance, slowly guiding himself inside me. He grips my hips, guiding me up and down on him as I continue to drink. I whimper from the sensation.

"Kane," I moan, biting down on him again. Each thrust sends waves of pleasure through me.

He shudders, tightening his hold on me. I pull back slightly, looking into his eyes, dark with need.

"Yes, baby, I'm yours," he groans, his voice rough. His fingers dig into my hips, guiding me faster, deeper.

I feel him nearing his peak. His release comes with a deep growl, and I welcome it, feeling his warmth fill me. I take a few more gulps of his blood until I'm satisfied.

Then, I carefully lick the wound, my saliva sealing it and leaving a permanent scar. A sense of victory washes over me —I've claimed him. I own him now. I pull back, a hand over my mouth as I realize what just happened. I start to panic, and he slides out of me, holding me close.

"It's okay, baby. What you did was natural." He gently sets me down and pulls me under the shower head, washing me from head to toe.

"I feel dizzy," I tell him. He smiles and continues washing me, keeping a hand at my waist to steady me. His smile is big, and I find myself getting lost in his green eyes once again.

Once finished, he turns off the shower, picks me up, and carries me out, grabbing a towel. He dries me off and dresses me in a nightdress and pajama pants. I look up at him nervously, biting my lip.

"You're not sleeping with me?" I ask, pouting. I need him now more than ever. He smiles and picks me up, carrying me to the bed.

"I need to take care of some things before we leave for the village in the morning," he says, setting me down gently and pulling the blanket over me, tucking me in. He strokes my cheek, and I let out a heavy yawn.

"Go to sleep, baby. I'm not going anywhere." He brushes his fingers over my claim mark. I sigh and yawn again, rolling to my side, my hand on my belly. Kane continues stroking my cheek until I finally fall asleep.

26

Kane

O nce I've finally got Tami calmed down and in bed, I quickly dress and head downstairs, remembering Kade is outside waiting for me. I pause by the door, brushing my fingers over my claim mark, feeling overjoyed.

Finally, my mate has claimed me, and we are complete. Suddenly, I feel my wolf relax within me. He wants to return to the village and settle our mate in. Was this why my wolf was so unhinged? He just wanted to be claimed?

I open the cabin door and walk past Kade standing on the porch with a grin that grates on my nerves. I know she heard Tami claim me, but I don't care. I also don't want to hear about it.

Kade follows me down the stairs and up the hill as I go to grab the trailer. I don't plan to unpack it since we'll be leaving for the village in the morning. It's winter, and the items will be safe in the trailer overnight. But I need to get it off the road.

"Why are you still here, Kade?" I ask, annoyed, as I start to pull the trailer back to the cabin. Kade walks with me.

"That's a nice claim mark. I'm always jealous of shifter claim marks. Shifters get the bigger bites. I just have a little scar," she says, running her fingers over her own claim mark.

She should be grateful for her mark, no matter the size. I don't care if it's a little scratch as long as Tami claimed me. I run my fingers over my mark again, feeling proud. I give Kade a hard glare, waiting for her to answer me.

"I need your help," Kade says.

My help? With what? I keep walking, pulling the trailer down the hill until we reach the cabin. I double-check the tarp to make sure it's secure.

The air is cool and thick, and there's another storm on the horizon. I can smell it in the air. This will make it difficult to travel in the morning, but I'll make it work. It's time to take Tami home. My brother is right; I've been selfish in keeping her here.

"The radicals have escalated," Kade says, helping me secure the tarp.

"Escalated?" Kade sighs and nods.

"While rescuing the human for your mate, we discovered some things. And it's not good."

"Tiffany?" I question, and Kade nods.

"There's an underground ring trafficking shifter babies. The fated mates that refuse to move into Wintermoon are falling victim to this. The mates are killed, and the children are sold off into an underground ring." I laugh, refusing to believe it. No way is something like this happening. *Fate would never allow it.*

"I don't understand it either, Kane. But it looks like it's part of Fate's plan."

"How are they even doing this? How does a radical kill a shifter?" I question, laughing. This has to be a mistake. There's no way... But I pause when Kade pulls a syringe from her pocket and hands it to me. Immediately, I get a whiff of lion shifter blood, but it's dead.

"They're draining shifter blood from the dead and injecting it into their bodies. It warms the dead blood, masking it and confusing the shifters enough to be infiltrated. I don't know all the details, but just enough to know it's happening. There are cubs and pups without families. You of all shifters know how that feels. You lost your parents in the Great War. A young shifter maneuvering the world on his own, solely relying on his wolf. Your wolf raised you."

"No, House of Zorah raised him. Don't put your maternal nonsense into his head." Levi reappears, cleaned up and in fresh clothes. He stands beside me, placing a hand on my shoulder. I give him a nod, signaling no hard feelings between us. He sees my claim mark and smiles.

"Ah, you are one with your mate now. Maybe I should give you another month alone with her," he says with a teasing smile. I shake my head.

"No, I need her surrounded by love. The village will provide that," I say, looking back at Kade. "What do you need from me?"

"We caught a radical posing as a tourist, thanks to Tiffany. They're going to try to take another pregnant mate. We tried to find Julian, but he's gone off the radar. You have his scent imprinted; I know you can help us find him." Levi takes the syringe.

"This is a call for the second Great War, Kade, and you know it," Levi tells her.

"We just got this land. Can't we settle in first before

everything goes to hell? Help me find the radicals and put this to rest quietly."

"No, we should tell King Amir," Levi disagrees.

"How many more shifter babies have to suffer while we wait?" Kade questions, shutting us up. I look at Levi, and he nods.

"Alright. Where's this radical human?" I ask, and Kade smiles.

"At the station on Mackinac Island. Just a quick ferry ride and a sniff, then you're back with your mate."

"I don't know," I say, suddenly having a bad feeling. I don't want to leave Tami alone. Kade looks up at the sky.

"The island is closed due to the winter storm and the roads are blocked. This will be quick, and you'll be back with your mate. I'll figure out the rest after I collect the scent." I look at Levi, and he nods.

"I'll go with you, brother," Levi says, but I'd rather he stay here with Tami. But I know my brother. He doesn't trust my wolf.

"Let's do this. You know I'm not staying away from my mate for long," I tell her.

"I'll teleport back routinely to check on her. I promise," Kade assures.

I don't have a good feeling about this, I don't know why. Julian, and Tami's avoidance about her phone, worry me. If she thinks I've forgotten, she's mistaken. I haven't given up the idea of searching for him myself.

"Help me get some of this food inside for my mate. She's carrying now, she'll be hungry." Kade smiles and nods, lifting the tarp.

Levi helps me carry the food inside while I dart upstairs to check on Tami. She's sleeping peacefully, her adorable little snores echoing through the room. I walk to the edge of the bed and gently stroke her cheek. She moans and turns to her side, moving away. I should leave her a note or something, but I'll be back before she wakes.

It's already agonizing just thinking about being away from her. It's going to be a long time before anyone can separate me from her. I draw in a breath, careful to be quiet. I have to do this. It's the right thing. And Tami would push me to go if she knew.

"I love you, Tami," I murmur. She stirs, rolling to her side to face me. She's still deeply asleep, her breathing slow and even. It's the first time I've let the words escape me. I've wanted to say them for weeks now, since the first time I laid eyes on her.

"I love you too," she murmurs back. My heart quickens at her words. I long to hear those words escape her lips when she's awake, but I'll take them coming from her sleep for now.

I make the painful walk out of our bedroom and go downstairs where Kade and Levi are waiting. I scowl at both of them; they look like proud parents. We head out of the cabin, and Levi is the last to exit, ensuring the door is locked.

The wolf in me and my brother won't let us leave without rounding the cabin, double-checking the perimeter. When I'm certain it's clear, I give Levi a nod that it's okay to leave. My heart feels heavy as I take the steps up the hilltop, leaving my mate alone.

I hope I don't regret this.

27

Tami

Hunger wakes me, and my eyes slowly flutter open. I weakly sit up in bed, yawning.

The cabin is quiet, too quiet. I slide out of bed and go to the window, bracing myself for the blood-covered snow as I peek outside.

Heavy snowflakes fill the air, covering the scene of Kane and Levi's battle earlier. My stomach rumbles again, and I place a hand on my belly. I smile, smoothing my hand over my abdomen.

"Okay, little one. Let's get you something to eat," I coo to our baby.

Once again, I'm feeling emotional. Where is Kane? Maybe he went out to hunt. My fingers immediately go to my lips as I remember what happened hours before.

I bit Kane—I claimed him. The mating process is complete between us. I own him and he owns me. I get to keep Kane forever. I get to keep our baby forever. I spent so long wondering if I'd ever have something like this. Yawning, I stretch out my arms and make my way to the stairs.

I hear something in the kitchen and smile. That must be Kane, already making me something to eat. There was a lot going on earlier, and we need to talk, especially about moving to his village in the morning. I don't like Levi. I don't like the way he treated Kane.

Right now, I just want to hold Kane. I know he's okay, but I still feel like I almost lost him. I dart down the stairs excitedly, giggling when I almost slip, but I catch myself.

Usually, Kane's on me in a heartbeat, scolding me for not being careful. This time, nothing. I steady myself, already feeling uneasy about who's in our kitchen.

When I reach the bottom of the stairs, I freeze. Julian's friend is on the sofa. I recognize him: Kamel, the one who pushed for Julian to take me.

How did he get in here? I close my eyes, praying I'm just having a nightmare. But when I open them and turn my head, I see Julian in the kitchen, making a sandwich.

My heart feels like it's about to burst out of my chest. My purse is on the counter, and everything is dumped out. Julian smiles when he meets my eyes.

"There you are sleepyhead. I wanted to pack some food for you before we left," he says as if it's just any day. He doesn't know he's messing with a woman mated to a shifter? He pulls a small device out of my wallet that looks like a GPS tracking device.

"You were the woman I chose, Tami. You think I wouldn't keep tabs on you? I watched you everywhere and listened. I heard everything for the past six weeks." He places a bottled water in front of the sandwich and gestures for me to sit.

"You got yourself knocked up by that shifter." He snarls, pointing at me. "You didn't want to give me a baby, but you'd let him knock you up."

"How are you here, and he not know?" I mutter nervously. Kamel stands from the sofa and approaches me, roughly gripping the back of my neck and pushing me toward the bar. He forces me to sit. Then he looks at Julian.

"They're on to us. This was a bad idea coming here for her."

"Shut up, Kamel. We're right on the border. She eats this sandwich and drinks this water, then we get out of here. You've seen how sick they get when they don't eat," Julian snaps.

"Eat this food so we can leave." Kamel presses a gun to my head. I immediately grab the sandwich and take a bite. Julian leans on the counter, his eyes cold.

"If you scream, I will blow your head off," Kamel threatens, pressing the gun to my temple. "Then your mate will have nothing." I nod, doing my best to finish the sandwich. I take the last bite, stuffing it into my mouth, then wash it down with water. Julian smiles.

"We've done this many times. We know pregnant mates can only drink water. And we know how to use your connection to your mate against you," Julian tells me. Kamel pulls a syringe from his pocket and hands it to Julian. Julian stabs himself with it.

"Shifter blood. It confuses them. It's how we got through the border without question. Wintermoon's population is growing. There are too many shifters to track. Easy for a radical to slip by."

"What are you going to do to me?" I question. Julian walks around the counter and roughly cups my face.

"First, I'm going to get rid of that bastard growing in you. It'll make us a pretty penny. Then, I'm going to lock you away and make you my main bitch. I'm a Brookstone. I get what I want, when I want," Julian growls.

"But you were with Tiffany." He laughs.

"I used her to get closer to you. My little loner CNA, who just works and goes home. You're not a woman I need to worry about running the streets. I need someone strong enough to give me babies and won't ask for me." His hand comes between my legs, and I wince, turning my head away. I didn't know he was a radical. I've heard him rant, but I never thought of him as a radical.

Radicals are the worst of humanity. They believe humans are at the top of the food chain and supernaturals are a threat to the natural way of life. They want supernaturals eradicated, not just hidden.

Radical politicians are on the rise, forming groups to fight against the supernaturals of Wintermoon. This is the safest place for supernaturals since there are no laws against killing them on human territory. Women's rights are fading, making human territory darker by the second.

Radicals hate supernaturals because many women seek Wintermoon for refuge. Everyone has heard the rumors of Wintermoon, how the women are treated here. And I've experienced it firsthand.

"This isn't worth it, Julian. I got a bad feeling," Kamel says, lowering his pistol. He steps back and walks to the cabin door, grabbing my coat and boots. Julian grips the back of my neck and pushes me toward the door, pushing me so hard I fall to my knees in front of Kamel.

"Put your coat and boots on. It's time to go," he growls.

Kamel raises the pistol, and fear courses through me. I

quickly slide into my boots and slowly rise to my feet, pulling on my coat. Julian grips the back of my neck, pushing me out of the cabin just as a large SUV pulls up. The driver moves to the passenger seat as Julian shoves me into the back and climbs in beside me.

Where is Kane? Will he hear me if I call for him? I have to do something. I can't let him take me out of Wintermoon and away from Kane.

"KANE! HELP ME!" I scream. Julian slaps me so hard I slam into the window.

"Shut up!" he growls, slamming the passenger door. Kamel jumps into the driver's seat, while another man, whom I don't recognize, sits in the front passenger seat, loading an automatic weapon.

"He won't hear you. I've got your mate distracted on the island. We're just five minutes from the border. We'll be back in Michigan in no time." Kamel puts the vehicle in reverse, moving up the hilltop, then turns onto the road.

The snow is coming down heavily, and visibility is low. Kamel maneuvers easily through the slippery road. I put my hand to my forehead, wincing from the pain of Julian's slap.

They're getting close to the border. I can partially make out the bridge through the snow. Is this how it ends for me? I should have known better; my life has never had a fairy tale ending.

This is why I never get attached to anything. It always gets snatched away when I get comfortable. I got comfortable with Kane. I felt safe and protected, but nothing can protect me from my destiny. It's to be with this monster of a man.

Why else would Fate let him take me? I start to sob quietly and rest my head against the window. I want to fight them, but I don't want them to hurt my baby. I'll figure out how to get out of this on my own, but I've got to play my cards right.

I'm a survivor. This is what I do: survive the worst situations I keep getting thrown into. I'll survive this, and I'll save our baby.

28

Kane

The moment the ferry left the docks, something felt off. And now I feel it again—*the pull*. I'm too far away from my mate.

But how? The docks are less than a mile from the cabin. It feels like Tami is running away from me. I put a hand to my chest, feeling a dreadful ache. Kade looks at me, raising an eyebrow.

"Your woman is in Wintermoon. How the hell are you feeling *the pull* now?" she grumbles, then falls silent. Without me needing to say the words, she immediately teleports off the ferry, leaving a black mystical cloud of smoke behind her.

She's back in less than a minute, and her expression confirms my suspicions. My mate is gone.

"Oh, shit!" Kade grits out. She's holding a syringe similar to the one she showed me earlier, only it's empty. Someone took my woman and my baby.

I start to gag, falling to my knees, feeling sick to my

stomach.

"This was all a distraction. To get us away from the cabin. Ah, fuck. I don't like being made a fool," Kade growls. She squeezes the syringe, crushing it.

"They're trying to take Tami across the bridge. If they succeed, it will be harder to get her back," Levi says as he helps me to my feet. I run to the edge of the ferry, ready to jump into the waters to go after my mate, but Levi stops me.

"The water is too cold for your wolf. You'll go into shock. Wait for the ferry to dock, and I'll help you kill those assholes," he urges.

I slap his hand away and try again, but this time Kade grabs me. I stiffen because I know what she can do. She'll teleport me off the ferry and it will render me unconscious. Levi immediately tells the crew to turn the ferry around.

"This is taking too long!" I growl.

"If I leave, you'll jump off the boat. I can't lose you, Tami, and the baby. Tami will never forgive me if I let you die trying to swim to her," Kade says.

I let out a growl, a monstrous, agonizing sound pleading with our Goddess Fate for mercy. I just got her, and now Fate wants to take her from me. Why? Is this my punishment for keeping her away from the village, where she would have been safe?

Levi feels my pain and immediately comes to my aid.

"I swear it, brother, you will not lose your mate. They will not get off this bridge."

"How did they get past the spikes? How did they know where to find her?" I growl, falling to my knees again.

The pull is agonizing. It feels like the band between us is being stretched to its limit. Now I understand why *the pull* drove King Amir to madness.

Kade teleports away again and I look at the waters,

watching the ferry move closer to Wintermoon's shoreline. Just a little more and I can go after her. Kade returns after a few minutes, holding a small chip.

"They've been tracking her. The radicals have invested in intel that's undetectable to us. I don't feel any radiation from this device." Kade looks at Levi and they share a knowing look.

"I told you; we should have gone to King Amir about this. It's time for the second Great War. The humans are already preparing for it. Are we going to sit around and wait to be blindsided again?" Levi grumbles.

"We just got this land. We haven't even broken real ground on it," Kade says, at a loss for words.

The prophecy that she would gather all the packs, prides, clans, and covens to lead us to a supernatural land where we could live in harmony seems short-lived now.

She doesn't want to go to King Amir because she knows he'll start the process of the war. Many will die, but the prophecy says we will prevail and become the natural rulers of this world.

"I just want Tami back. I don't care about a prophecy. Can't you teleport to her? Please, just leave me and go get my woman." Kade looks at me with a pained expression, then looks into the cloudy night sky.

I'm begging Fate to have mercy on me right now. I see the error of my ways, my selfishness to keep Tami close and away from my village and the supernaturals of Wintermoon.

I'll change. I'll be a better mate to my woman and our child. I'll do anything, just please don't take her from me. I put my face in my hands, desperate to escape the agony of losing the one thing that gave my life meaning.

"Kane," Levi says with a sigh, gently placing his hand on my shoulder. I don't push him away.

I know he understands the extent of my pain. I can feel *the pull,* the invisible band that keeps us together. It doesn't matter where they take her, *the pull* will help me find her.

These radicals can't keep her from me. I should have taken her to my brother's village and hunted Julian when I had the chance. I knew he was a problem from the beginning, I could sense it.

"Leah, any day now!" Kade growls. A mystical cloud of smoke reappears, and Leah steps into view.

"They're getting close to the border. I called Gabriel and a few others from surrounding clans, packs, and prides. They won't get past the bridge, I assure you," Leah says. "You should let me..."

"No, Leah. You've done enough. Now, will you please speed up this boat so Kane can get to his mate before I have to teleport him?" Leah looks at me, lets out a sympathetic sigh, and shrugs.

"Fine! You all are no fun. I could have used a kill. And I want to get to know Tami better." She pouts, moving to the edge of the boat. Her fingers dance over the water, and suddenly, the boat surges forward.

The water beneath us shifts, swirling from deep blue to vibrant emerald, laced with streaks of silver as Leah's magic pulses through it.

Leah's connection to the craft is strong, her power undeniable. Kade's abilities are different. While she no longer shares the same connection to the craft as her wife, she can teleport and control the elements.

As the boat speeds up, every second feels like an eternity. I need my mate back. I need her in my arms.

Just when I sense I'm close enough to the shoreline, I immediately shift into my wolf form.

My muscles tense, and heat surges through my veins.

Bones crack and reshape beneath my skin. Fur bursts forth, covering my body in a thick coat. My senses sharpen—the scent of the forest, the sound of waves crashing nearby, all become vivid and clear.

"Kane!" Levi yells, but I ignore him.

My wolf leaps off the boat, aiming to land on the docks. He barely makes it, his back legs dropping into the water while he claws at the docks, pulling himself out.

The water is ice cold, a shock to his body as Levi warned, but it's not enough to stop him from getting to our woman. My wolf manages to climb up the dock and takes off, running into the forest.

I can hear Levi right behind us, his wolf catching up as my wolf maneuvers through the trees. My wolf pushes hard, moving faster, cutting through the forest. We're never leaving Tami alone again!

Julian is a dead man when my wolf catches him. He's going to rip Julian's head from his body and feast on his flesh.

How will Tami feel about this? Will she still love me once she sees the darker, more sinister side of my wolf as he kills in her honor? My wolf wants to present Julian's head to her as a gift, to show our love and devotion, putting it on full display for her.

When this is over, I'm taking Tami to the village, where she'll stay until I calm down. I don't know how long it will take—weeks, months, possibly years.

We are on the road within minutes, and my wolf stops, taking in the tire tracks, which are quickly being covered by the snow. Levi's wolf stops and howls into the night sky. I know what he's doing; he's calling for help.

My wolf takes off running, following the quickly disappearing tire tracks as the snow picks up. Visibility is low due to the storm, but he keeps pushing through, desperate to get our woman back.

The only thing on his mind is blood and vengeance, to show these radicals what happens when you try to take a mate from a mate.

And I won't stop until we get it.

29

Tami

Julian's hand crashes against my face, harder than before, jolting me. My head snaps back, hitting the window with a sickening thud. Blood fills my mouth, and I instinctively cover my face, shrieking as I turn away from him.

"Once we cross this bridge, you're going to regret ever choosing that shifter over me," he snarls. "You'll wish you never crossed me, you stupid bitch."

"Fate chose me the moment I was born!" I snap back, but Julian slaps me again. My head slams against the window, and everything blurs.

As we approach the bridge, my heart aches with the thought of never seeing Kane again. I'm determined to fight for our baby, to ensure they have the life I never did. I'll do whatever it takes to get back to Wintermoon.

I rest my head against the window, feeling the impact echo in my skull every time I move.

Sadness weighs me down as we near the exit, and I can't

help but wonder what's next for me. Suddenly, something catches my eye. I blink, squinting into the trees. There it is again—a dark figure leaping from branch to branch.

Hope surges in my chest. Is it Kane, racing through the trees to save me? I keep quiet, glancing at Julian, who suddenly looks uneasy. We're getting closer to the bridge, and I know it won't be long before we hit the border.

A shadow suddenly looms over the truck, its massive wings flapping loudly, blocking out the moonlight. A monstrous screech slices through the air above us.

"Shit! What the hell is that?" Julian exclaims, glancing around. He rolls down his window and leans out, eyes wide, but whatever he sees makes him pull back in a panic, quickly rolling the window up.

"Kamel, step on it!" he shouts, yanking his pistol from its holster and checking the chamber.

Relief washes over me. Kane must have sent help. He won't let me get off this bridge, and I'm grateful for it.

Suddenly, a massive, scaly dragon lands in front of the bridge, blocking our escape.

Its venomous green eyes glare at us, sharp teeth gleaming in the moonlight, and thick talons digging into the ground. I scream at the sight, but Kamel keeps the accelerator pressed down.

"They won't hurt us. We have their bitch; they won't let anything happen to her," Kamel says, his voice steady as he floors the gas. The dragon roars, fire erupting from its chest, creating a line of flames that scorches the snow.

Still, Kamel doesn't hesitate. He pushes forward, racing through the fire, drawing closer to the dragon.

Suddenly, a figure leaps from the shadows of the trees, landing right in front of us, arm outstretched, palm up. But Kamel keeps driving, bracing himself for impact.

"No! Get out of the way!" I scream, but Julian slaps me hard again, and my head crashes against the window.

The truck flips over the man, and I brace myself against the ceiling. I scream along with Julian, Kamel, and the other passenger. The truck hangs in the air, flipping for what feels like forever before it finally slams back onto its tires, my head jerking forward to hit the driver's seat.

Before Kamel can hit the gas, the driver's side door is ripped off its hinges. A massive hand reaches in, grabbing Kamel by the neck and yanking him out of the truck. He screams while I hold my forehead, trying to shake off the impact.

Julian suddenly grabs the back of my neck, dragging me out through the back passenger door. I spit out the blood pooling in my mouth as I hit the ground.

Pain shoots through my body, and I instinctively touch my abdomen, worry flooding my mind about the baby.

Julian wraps an arm around my throat and presses the pistol to my temple, pulling me around the truck. A man stands tall ahead of us, rugged yet refined, with high cheekbones and a strong jaw. His skin is a deep mahogany, smooth and flawless.

His icy blue eyes seem to see right through me, framed by shoulder-length dreadlocks that sway in the breeze. He's muscular, exuding strength, yet his posture is relaxed. He's shirtless, wearing only sweatpants, his bare feet sinking into the snow. His large hands are clenched at his sides.

He looks so much like Kane that I can't help but wonder if he's another one of his brothers. He meets my gaze, gives a slight smile, and nods. Suddenly, the front passenger door swings open, and the man inside leaps out, sprinting into the forest. He must know he's a dead man for this.

"Let her go, and I'll make it quick," the tall man says, low and growling. But Julian doesn't relent. He keeps the pistol pressed hard against my temple, his grip tightening around my throat as he drags me away.

The dragon's roar startles me, sending fear coursing through my veins. The man raises his hand to the massive creature, signaling it to stop.

"Stop, you're scaring our princess," he says, and the dragon huffs, silencing its roar.

"Back off!" Julian yells, pressing the pistol harder against my head.

"You aren't crossing the bridge with her. She's a princess of Wintermoon," the man replies, stepping forward. I wince as Julian squeezes my throat tighter, cutting off my air. I start to gag, and the man pauses.

"I'm not letting her go until I'm across the bridge," Julian yells, his pistol pointed at my head with a shaky hand. Just then, a cloud of black smoke rises behind us. I grin, knowing exactly who it is.

Kade appears, knocking the gun from Julian's hand and freeing my throat. I drop to my knees as Kade lunges at Julian, sending him crashing into the snow. Kade pulls me up.

"I've got you, little princess," she says, lifting me and cradling me against her chest. The man brushes his fingers over my forehead.

"The baby is fine. The heartbeat is strong," he murmurs. He meets my gaze briefly before looking away.

"I'm Gabriel, sister. I hate that we had to meet this way, but it's a pleasure to welcome you to the pack. Welcome to Wintermoon."

Two large, black-furred wolves leap from the trees. I recognize them immediately.

"Kane!" I call weakly, reaching out my bloody hand. The

silver-eyed wolf shifts into Levi, who stands beside Gabriel. Kane stays in wolf form, moving closer and brushing his snout against mine.

Julian scrambles to his feet and bolts for the bridge, but the dragon's tail swings and knocks him down, sending him sliding through the snow. He struggles to get up and then disappears into the forest.

Kade looks back at me with a smile.

"No more mates on the border," she jokes. I lean my head against her chest, too tired to respond.

"She's fine, Kane. A little banged up, but your baby is strong," Kade assures him.

"How about a kill in your mate's honor?" Kade suggests, and Kane's wolf howls into the night sky in agreement.

Gabriel leaps into the forest, and within seconds, I hear Julian's screams as Gabriel drags him out and drops him in front of Kane.

My eyes shift to a large SUV speeding across the bridge, blocking the entrance before cutting the engine. Damon and Tristian step out, approaching us slowly.

Relief washes over me, and I start to sob against Kade's chest, desperate to return home to Kane. Kane's wolf whimpers at my cries, and Kade gently rubs my back.

"Don't cry, princess. You're in good hands now," Kade says. Damon gives the dragon's tail a pat, and it suddenly leaps into the air, flying off into the night. I had no idea dragon shifters existed.

"Looks like the radicals are escalating," Damon says, gripping Julian by the neck and lifting him like a rag doll. Julian kicks and screams for help as Damon holds him in front of me.

"You're sheriffs of Wintermoon! You have to return me to

Michigan law officials!" Julian yells. "Do you know who my family is?" Damon laughs, still gripping him.

"Brookstone, we've dealt with your bloodline before. You're trespassing in Wintermoon; your laws don't apply here," Damon replies, dropping Julian to his knees in front of Kane's wolf. Kane's wolf growls, saliva pooling as it bares its teeth just inches from Julian's face.

"You broke Fate's biggest law. You can't take a mate from a mate. Fate will never allow it," Kade says, smiling.

"You're the police! You can't just let them kill me! My family will come for me!" Julian screams, but fear flickers in his eyes. I tighten my grip on Kade, watching Julian beg for his life.

I'm watching Kade look around, confusion on her face. "I don't see anything but pack business. Do you see anything, Damon?" she asks. Damon stuffs his hands in his pockets, whistling as he heads over to Julian's truck, climbing into the driver's seat and starting the engine.

"I'll need their heads to deliver to the police," he calls from the doorless seat.

"See, Levi? I can handle this without King Amir's help, and I know how to mind pack business," Kade teases, and Levi growls back at her.

"Two of them have a head start. Looks like we have our hunt for the night," Gabriel says to Levi.

They share a knowing glance before leaping into the forest, heading in opposite directions. Kane's wolf growls, getting closer as Julian starts to back away.

"Why is Tami so important to you, Julian? You should have left her when you found out she was mated. Now, you're a dead man," Kade says, stepping around Julian while carrying me to the side. Tristian steps forward, smiling at me.

"Everything is going to be alright, little lady," Tristian says.

"Goodbye, Julian. May the other radicals be smarter than you," Kade adds.

Kane's wolf lunges at Julian, sinking its teeth into his flesh. I watch as blood splatters onto the white snow, painting it red. Julian screams, choking as Kane's wolf tears into him. I can't look away as the wolf bites down hard, ripping Julian's head off and tossing it at Kade's feet.

"Look, a gift from your wolf," Kade says with a smile. That's all I remember before my eyelids grow heavy, and sleep takes over. I can still hear Kane's wolf howl into the night.

30

Kane

Tami's been sleeping for hours, and I'm starting to worry. Our baby's heartbeat is strong and well protected in her womb. Finally, she starts to stir when I gently caress her cheek.

I've been trying to coax her awake for hours. I need to make sure she eats and gets plenty of water in her system, not only for the baby but for herself. Pregnancy is tough on the body, and she'll experience many changes while our baby grows inside her.

I brought her back to my home village instead of the cabin where our love first blossomed.

Kade is right; that is no place for a mate. Gabriel stands against the wall, keeping watch over her. Funny, he doesn't have this overprotective stance for Micah and Levi's mates, just mine. Some strange wolf claim he's taken on her.

"I can take care of my mate, Gabriel. I don't need you hovering over her," I snap, but he stands there, arms firmly folded over his chest. He's the last of our pack left, waiting for a mate.

"You left your pregnant mate to be captured by human radicals. You can't convince me you know how to properly care for her. She needs a protector, and she'll have one until the child is born." I growl and stand from the bed, getting right in my brother's face. He maintains his posture, unbothered by my intimidating stance. He smiles.

"Shall we take this outside, brother?" Gabriel offers, flashing his canines in a smug grin.

A black cloud of mystical smoke appears in the room, making us pause, and Kade and Leah appear before us, Leah holding several bags of clothes and food. I don't need their help with my mate. I've got it.

I growl in irritation, stepping back from my brother and returning to Tami, who's still sleeping soundly. She moans from the noise, turning to her side.

"Stop blaming Kane for this, Gabriel," Kade says, walking over to the rocking chair I carved and relaxing in it. She smiles, making herself comfortable. "This one is far nicer than the one I took a couple of months ago."

"Why are you here?" I growl, returning to my mate. I sit at the edge of the bed, gently stroking her back.

"That's no way to greet us, Kane. We're only here to check on the both of you. This was traumatic for all of us. Never did we think the radicals would get this far in infiltrating our land." Leah chides me, setting the bags down on the dresser.

"I think Levi is right. We should alert King Amir about this. We are being infiltrated. They've increased their technologies and are injecting dead shifter blood to muffle out the scent. We can't hide this from him.

How many supernaturals are victims of this genocide?"

Gabriel interrupts, stepping forward. He walks to the edge of the bed, folding his arms over his chest, guarding Tami like a watchdog. I growl at him. Will he get out of my room and let me care for my woman?

Gabriel has always been like this, the certified watchdog of our village. I want him gone and far away from me and my mate, but that's not going to happen unless Gabriel finds a greater cause to serve. Right now, that cause is Tami, my woman. Uggh! I've never been more irritated.

"We have it handled, Gabriel. And we're taking a little trip into Detroit's underground to find out how deep this rabbit hole goes. We can't save every supernatural. They have to come here willingly, but we can stop the trafficking. With your help, of course." Kade says, and Gabriel looks at her, his blue eyes pondering. I can tell he's up for the challenge.

"I need to stay here until the baby is born. This is a child of the House of Zorah. We've waited centuries for a family unit. It's here now, and I won't let anyone take it from us." Gabriel declines, but I can see it in his eyes. He wants to take the offer, and I want him to take it. This is one of the many reasons why I never wanted to bring my mate here. I can see it now, Gabriel always hovering, and I won't get a moment alone with my woman.

Tami moans again and turns her back on the bed, her eyes slowly fluttering open. She immediately takes her hand to her forehead, wincing. Kade starts to pull her sleeve to bite into her wrist, but I stop her.

"I do not want vampire blood in my mate while she's pregnant. Her wounds will heal quickly now that she's fully mated with me." I state, halting her. Kade groans and relaxes in her chair. Leah sits on the bed and gently strokes Tami's cheek.

"Wake up, sleepyhead," she teases, flashing her fangs.

Tami looks at her and winces, then slowly starts to sit up. I immediately come to her side, helping her prop some pillows against the headboard so she can relax. We keep quiet, letting the memories of what happened last night come back to her.

She gasps, and panic finally sets in as she looks around nervously, her eyes meeting mine.

"Kane!" she yelps, then throws her arms around me. I embrace her, holding her tight until she pulls away, gently cupping my face, tears welling in her eyes.

"I thought I was going to be lost to you forever." She says, and I smile, letting her kiss me tenderly.

"I should never have left you. That won't happen again, I assure you." Tami presses her forehead against mine for a long moment, taking a deep breath. I can feel her relief.

"I should have told you what was in my phone before you crushed it. Julian sent me a text. He said he knew where I was and that he was going to find me." She murmurs, but I shake my head.

"It doesn't matter, Tami. None of it matters. I should never have left you alone. I'll have to live with that regret forever."

"What matters is that you're alright, Tami." Leah says, sitting on the bed. She reaches out and gently strokes Tami's back as I hold her.

Tami crawls into my lap, straddling me. She clings to me, burying her face in my neck, nuzzling her nose against my claim mark. Now is not the time for my arousal, but it's happening anyway.

"Kane!" Leah and Kade both shout as soon as they catch a whiff of my arousal. Gabriel remains against the wall, snickering.

"Baby, stop. Bad timing." I say. She pulls back with a giggle when she feels my shaft pressing against her.

She looks around the room, taking in the surroundings. Leah stands from the bed and grabs a food tray, opening it and sliding it over to her with utensils.

Hunger hits Tami the moment she smells her meal. She climbs off me and pulls the tray into her lap. I want to pull her back, but I'm just happy she's eating. Leah grabs the pitcher of ice water on the end table and pours Tami a glass, holding it out to her, but

Tami takes the pitcher instead, leaving Leah holding the glass. She downs the pitcher in a few gulps, clearly thirsty. When she's finished, she belches, running her hand over her mouth.

"Sorry," she mumbles, staring at the empty pitcher. Leah smiles and takes it from Tami, then hands her the glass.

"I'll go get you a refill," Leah says, leaving the room. Kade pulls the small tracking device from her pocket, pinching it between two fingers.

"Julian has been watching you for a long time. There's no telling how much intel he's sold. He knew about the spikes, and with the shifter blood injections, he crossed into Wintermoon undetected. We have a serious problem." Kade murmurs, and Tami quickly looks up from her food.

"I didn't know. I'm so sorry. I would never..."

"No one is blaming you, baby." I interrupt, glaring at Kade. If she's here to make my woman feel worse, I won't let it happen.

"Of course not," Kade assures. "I'm not here to blame your mate, Kane. But we need to talk. Tami needs to stay on Wintermoon, no traveling, unless it's to Mackinac Island. You killed Julian Brookstone, a human from an affluent family. They want vengeance for his death. While we're dealing with that, I need to figure out how they built this chip and where it comes from."

"They said they were going to sell my baby on the black market," Tami announces. A low growl rumbles from my chest, echoed by Gabriel.

"No one is taking your baby, Tami. You are a princess of the House of Zorah." Gabriel declares.

"And a daughter of Wintermoon," Kade finishes, causing Gabriel to roll his eyes.

Leah returns with a new pitcher of water, setting it on the end table. She stands beside Kade.

"We'll leave you two alone. Welcome to Wintermoon, Tami. I know you'll love the village." Leah says.

Kade stuffs the small device in her pocket. They teleport out of the room, leaving their signature cloud of black mystical smoke lingering in the air. I watch it slowly evaporate, then look at Gabriel, giving him a hard glare.

"A little privacy, Gabriel." I growl. Heaving a sigh, he drops his hands to his sides and steps toward the bed.

"Do you remember me, little princess?" He asks Tami. She shrugs.

"Yes, a little. You made the truck flip. Thank you for saving me." Gabriel smiles.

"You're my sister now. I'm always going to protect you. And you're carrying a child for the House of Zorah." Gabriel looks at me with a hard glare, then back to Tami.

"Since your mate was careless and left you alone, it's my duty to ensure you have proper protection during your pregnancy."

"Um... Thanks, but Kane can..." I grab her hand, stopping her.

"There's no use in declining. Gabriel's decision is final.

He's decided to be your watchdog during your pregnancy."
Tami sighs, clearly overwhelmed.

"We are in the village, which is heavily protected. Get
out of my room, Gabriel." He snickers, his eyes lingering on
my mate for a moment, then leaves the room, quietly closing
the door behind him.

Tami pushes the food away and throws herself into my
arms. I hold her tight.

"So, we're in the village now?" She asks, and I nod.

"As soon as you're well, I'll introduce you to the sisters of
House of Zorah. Skylar is Micah's mate, and Nia is Levi's
mate. Nia is the Luna of our pack, but she doesn't care much
for the position." I tell her. Tami sighs and presses her forehead against mine.

"I'm so sorry, baby. I should never have left you alone."
Tami shakes her head.

"No, you can't blame yourself for this. I won't let you. You
came for me, and you saved me. I'm the happiest woman in
the world right now." My heart warms at her words. My
hand moves from her waist, resting on her belly.

"I'm not leaving you or our baby alone again. I don't care
what the circumstances are." Tami squeezes me tight and
kisses my cheek.

"I love you, Kane." She whispers in my ear. I pull her
back and look into her eyes, smiling.

"I love you too, Tami." She smiles sleepily, and I pick her
up, gently placing her back on the bed and pulling the tray
into her lap. She returns to eating, and I watch her, thinking
of the wonderful life we will build together.

I'm thankful Fate didn't take her from me. But something
tells me Fate used Tami to alert Kade of what's coming.

That's how Fate works. She always places us in the right

situations. Maybe that's why I couldn't leave the cabin by the border—because Fate wasn't finished with me.

Now that I have Tami right where she belongs, I won't let anyone take her from me. She's mine forever, and I'll kill anyone who tries.

31

Tami

Six Months Later—Mackinac Island

I'm wobbling through Mackinac Island on a hot summer day, heavily pregnant despite Kane and Gabriel's protests.

I need a break from the village; sometimes their overwhelming love gets to me. Skylar and Nia are like sisters, and I've grown to love them too. Nia's a mother now, and Skylar is expecting our due dates just a month apart.

Wintermoon is my home. I can't imagine being anywhere else. But today, I have something else in mind. I asked Kade to help make Angie a lottery winner. I know she and her kids are here somewhere, and I want to find her. But Gabriel and Kane are practically caging me in.

After about ten minutes of walking, I stop to rest my belly. Kane growls at me, clearly unhappy that I'm out here instead of relaxing on the sofa with my feet up.

"Can I carry you now?" Kane mumbles, and I shake my head. I'm really enjoying this treatment; they spoil me. He growls as I start walking again, and Gabriel quietly follows.

Gabriel is a wild card. He's overly protective and never backs down from a fight. When he says he's watching me, he means it. The moment I step away from the village, he's right behind me. He doesn't complain about where I go as long as he's by my side.

We walk a bit longer until I pause in front of the diner next to the bakery where Leah works sometimes.

Kane looks ready to throw me over his shoulder if I keep this up, but then I spot Angie sitting by the window with her four kids, enjoying their vacation. I glance up at Kane and smile.

I adjust my purse and take slow steps across the street, heading for the diner.

Surprisingly, Gabriel stays behind, leaning against a trailer. He's eating another bag of strawberries, something he seems to do a lot. Kane presses his palm against my lower back, escorting me into the diner.

The patrons fall quiet for a moment when they see Kane's towering figure. Angie and her children look around and, when she catches a glimpse of me, she smiles and stands from her seat. I wobble over to her and Angie pulls me into a warm hug, then smooths her hand over my belly.

"Look at you," Angie coos, "I knew you'd be wobbling pregnant if I ever saw you again." She teases. I laugh. She places her hands on her hips, giving me a knowing look.

"Let me guess, my lottery ticket wasn't a coincidence." She says, and I give her a nervous laugh. She looks at Kane and smiles.

"You're mated to one of the big ones. That means big

babies." Kane smiles and wraps an arm around my waist, keeping me close.

"I wanted you to have your dreams." I tell her, and I see Leah walking by from the bakery, right on time. She enters the diner and approaches me, flashing a smile with her fangs. It catches Angie off guard. She's never seen a real vampire before.

"What are you doing out of the village? I told you I had it handled." Leah chides but kisses me on the cheek. She looks at Angie, who takes a nervous step back.

"Oh, there's nothing to fear with me, Angie. I'm Leah. I run Wintermoon with my wife, Kade, who's the sheriff of Wintermoon." She holds out a folder for Angie to take.

"Tami told me you are an excellent cook. We could use more good chefs on the island, that is if you're interested." Angie stares at me in awe and slowly takes the folder from Leah.

"We pay room and board, and ensure your children get the best education. It's a win-win."

"Oh, my god," Angie says, as if she can't believe it.

"I can come visit sometimes." I say, but Kane just growls at me. Angie looks at him with a smile.

"Tami, I don't know how to thank you. And before, when I was rude to you about being fated to Wintermoon..." I shake my head at her. I try to move forward to pull her into another hug, but Kane stops me, pushing me back behind him. Something's off. Even Leah's acting weird suddenly. They've caught the scent of something.

"Would you mind taking that outside, please? My family and I are trying to enjoy a meal, and you've got this big shifter with his bitch, stinking up the diner!" a man growls. Oh no, a radical. Why do they keep coming here if they hate us so much?

"Tami, say goodbye to Angie and go outside and stand with Gabriel." Leah says. I start to argue, but when Kane growls again, I quickly run to Angie and pull her into a tight hug, my belly bumping against her.

"Here, take this. Kane gave it to me a while ago, but he insists on paying for everything. I have no use for the money," I tell her, placing the cash in her hand. Angie looks at me with a loving smile.

"You saved me, Tami. I can't thank you enough." I shrug. I couldn't save Tiffany. Kade told me after she rescued her, she went right back to the same crowd. So, all this for nothing. But at least I could help Angie.

"Get your kids and get out of here. Everything you need is in that folder to get the employment process started." I tell her.

The angry man starts to shout at Leah while she does her best to try to calm him down. Angie quickly gathers her children, and they make their exit along with several other patrons who realize the situation has become hostile. I tug on Kane's arm, trying to get him to leave.

"He called you a bitch. I'm not leaving until I deal with him." Kane says, not looking at me. I run a hand through my hair, wondering if there's any way I can get Kane to leave with me. I tug at him again, but he remains unmoving.

"Don't antagonize a wolf shifter. You're asking for trouble!" Leah warns the man, but he doesn't listen. He stands and throws off his hat.

"You supernaturals think you can just take everything! This is our land; you belong in the shadows. This is human land!" he growls, getting in Leah's face. She may look small and frail, but she's far from it. Every supernatural on Wintermoon knows better.

"Tami, go outside, now!" she growls, and I huff, trying to

tug Kane again before giving up. I storm out of the diner in frustration, wobbling over to Gabriel, who's still leaning against the trailer, enjoying his bag of strawberries.

"It's pointless for Leah to reason with them. Those radicals are stiff-necked idiots. They can't see beyond their own beliefs," Gabriel mutters, biting into a strawberry.

"Why do you eat so many strawberries all the time?" I ask him in a huff, folding my arms over my chest. I'm irritated. I could only speak to Angie for a few minutes. But she'll be working on the island full-time soon, so I guess that means I get to see her more. She won't be able to travel into Wintermoon since she's not fated to anyone there.

Gabriel holds a strawberry out to me, and I take it.

"I have this theory that Fate has been preparing us for our fated mates all along. We thought she gave up on us when the curse was cast, but she never did. I'm attached to this fruit because it's the scent my mate holds." He says, then he touches the tip of my nose. "You, little princess, smell like fresh country apples. With a scent so strong like that, your bloodline must be from Kenya or Southwest Cameroon. My mate is most likely from South Africa or maybe even Egypt. With Fate, we're always placed in situations we don't understand until the time is right." I nod and take a bite of the strawberry. Gabriel grabs my arm and stands upright, pulling me behind him.

"Incoming," he says. Suddenly, the glass in the diner shatters and a man comes flying out, sliding across the cement toward us. Gabriel places his foot on the man's shoulder, stopping him.

"When will you radicals learn?" Gabriel says, shaking his head. Leah runs out of the diner, clearly irritated as Kane steps through the broken window. I huff, frustrated because he's making a scene.

"Don't panic everyone, it's just a minor disagreement!" Leah shouts at the crowd of humans taking photos and video footage. He walks past Leah with a smug smile, crossing the street while she puts a finger to her lips, wondering what to do next.

"Kade!" Leah shouts into the air. Kane steps over the man, screaming in pain as shards of glass pierce his skin. Kane walks around Gabriel, who's guarding me and pulls me into his arms.

"Kane!" I chide him, but he ignores me, pulling me against his chest.

"He had it coming, Tami," Gabriel says, defending Kane.

"He called you a bitch. He's lucky to be alive." Kane says, kissing my forehead.

"Well, will you three get off the island now?" Leah mutters, then she fans her hand over the large broken window. Hues of blue and gray sparkle over the window as the glass leaves the ground, returning to its place.

The man screams as the glass pieces fly out of his body and back into the window. The broken glass repairs itself, leaving only blood streaks from the man's injuries. Leah pulls a cloth from her apron and cleans the window.

"See, all done! Nothing to worry about." Leah says, and the crowd cheers at her display of magic. Kade suddenly teleports in front of us, leaving a black mystical cloud of smoke behind her. She grips the man by the collar of his shirt, lifting him effortlessly. He looks like a bodybuilder and is twice her size, yet she holds him as if he's nothing.

"Radicals," she mutters, shaking her head. "If I could ban them from the island, I would. But there's a no discrimination clause."

I cling to Kane while Gabriel snickers, biting into another strawberry. He's clearly enjoying this.

"But I can ban you from the island. We don't mistreat our women here." Kade smiles, flashing her fangs at the man. He starts to kick and pull at her, trying to get away in fear.

"Fucking vampire! This is our land! You can't just come here and take our land." Kade laughs.

"That's rich, coming from a lineage of colonizers. That's what your people have been doing for centuries. You're only reaping the benefits of that. Entitled humans." Kade looks at me with a wink.

Leah places her hands on her hips, giving Kade a hard glare. She sighs and starts to carry the man off, still holding him by his collar, heading for the police station. Leah crosses the street and approaches us, and Gabriel immediately stands aside.

"I'm sorry, Tami. He should not have spoken to you that way." I shrug. I'm not offended. I've been called worse things growing up in Detroit.

But it's nice to know I have protection here. Kane smooths his hand over my belly, and our baby boy starts to kick from his touch. Already in the womb, Kane's bonded with our baby. I can't wait to see the two of them together, watching as Kane teaches our son how to be a man.

"Let's go home." I say, and Kane scoops me into his arms.

"No more walking. That's enough for one day." Kane mutters, then starts down the hill, carrying me back to the ferry. Gabriel matches his pace, walking with us.

I relax against Kane and just enjoy his embrace, feeling the safest I've ever felt.

32

Kane

Nine Months Later—House of Zorah

My son coos against my chest as I prepare breakfast. I have him in a baby wrap, held snugly against me while he gnaws on his teething ring, his vibrant green eyes staring up at me with love.

Tami's still sleeping, which isn't surprising since she's pregnant again, but I'm not going to tell her just yet. It's bad to tell a woman before her body catches up with her. Her scent is different, a mix of fresh country apples and cherries. Maybe this time it's a girl?

I smile when I hear Tami's footsteps as she climbs out of bed and goes into the bathroom to brush her teeth.

Then she slips into a pair of slippers and makes her way downstairs, finding us in the kitchen. She's truly a vision. She scratches her head and looks around, a bit irritated that

I didn't wake her. Why would I? She's growing another baby; I can handle everything for now.

Bringing her back to my village is something I should have done from the beginning. Tami thrives here among the pack and fits right in as part of the family.

We gather twice a month in our village community center that Levi constructed, ensuring we congregate as a family instead of staying holed up in our cabins, which we all prefer.

Gabriel lets himself in through the front door, dusting his bare feet off from the snow, before entering the kitchen. He pats Tami gently on the forehead as he enters, then goes for what he came for, our son, Ocran. He pulls him out of the baby wrap, then sits down at the table.

Tami goes over to the coffee pot to make herself a cup of coffee, and I snicker. She's about to find out. She fixes her coffee the way she likes it, more cream and sugar than coffee, then takes a sip. Her face contorts with disgust, and she hurries to the sink to spit it out, wiping her mouth.

"This coffee has gone bad. I can't drink this crap!" she snaps. Realization hits her, and she glares at both me and Gabriel.

"You could have given me a heads up!" she snaps, pouring out her coffee. She folds her arms over her chest, frustrated.

"So, it's back to only water again. Ugh! That's the one thing I hate about being pregnant. Only water. Always water," she grumbles. I pull her into my arms, and she doesn't protest, resting her head against my chest.

"It's bad to tell a woman she's pregnant before she figures it out on her own," I say. She sighs and shrugs, her hands going to her belly. I can tell from her scent that she's ecstatic about being pregnant again, even though she's being moody. Tami wants this baby. She looks over at Gabriel, who's playing with Ocran.

"I just wanted to see him one more time before I leave. Hopefully, I'm back before your new baby is born," Gabriel says. Tami pulls away from me, wondering what he's talking about.

"You're leaving?" she asks.

"I told Kade I wouldn't help with the radicals until after Ocran was born. He's here now, so I need to keep my word. Plus, I feel something pulling me there. My mate, perhaps?" he says with a wink.

Tami's bonded well with my brothers, especially Gabriel. I can tell she doesn't want him to leave, but she's not going to protest him searching for his mate and stopping the radicals from harming other supernaturals.

Levi feels the same. He doesn't want Gabriel to leave, but who are we to stop Gabriel from finding his mate? He's the last of our pack without a mate, and I know it's getting to him.

When Levi and Micah found their mates, it was unbearable in the village. I can only imagine what Gabriel is going through.

"Have you told Levi?" I ask, scraping the eggs onto a large platter that has hashbrowns, bacon, and biscuits.

Tami steals a slice of bacon before grabbing plates and utensils, placing them at the table while I carry the platter. She tries to sit in her own chair, but I pull her into my lap.

"He's not happy about it," Gabriel answers, then reaches for a plate to serve himself while Ocran steals some food before he can even get a bite. I keep a firm grip on Tami, making sure she stays on my lap. She giggles, not fighting me. I tangle my fingers in her natural curls while she digs into her food.

"How long? Levi wants to start breaking ground on King Amir's palace," I ask. I'm not much of an architect; my skills are in carpentry, but I help whenever I can.

When Levi breaks ground on the palace, we'll all have to move our village temporarily to the island until it's finished. Tami and the other mates already dislike the seclusion in the village, so they are really going to hate being secluded on the island for a couple of years. But we'll find ways to balance things out and keep them happy. We always do.

"Until the situation is handled. I looked at the files. It's a lot worse than it looks. They're selling our children on the black market. We're going to put a stop to it and rescue them. Leah's already talking to Levi about building an orphanage for the children we rescue," Gabriel says.

"Oh my gosh," Tami says, and I can smell the heartache in her scent. She looks at Ocran, who doesn't have a care in the world, and feels blessed.

"I want to help with the orphanage. I have experience as a CNA, I'm sure my skills are needed," she offers, and I squeeze her tighter.

"Your skills are always needed, sister," Gabriel says with a smile, and I glare at him.

Does he not smell that she's pregnant? I don't want her doing anything but growing our baby. I almost lost my mind while she was pregnant with Ocran. Tami was always busy, on the move.

Angie had to explain to her that she's in a different place now and can't mingle with humans the way she used to. It took her a while, but she got over it. Now, she's settled into Wintermoon and hasn't looked back.

"Worry about the baby you're carrying first," Gabriel tells her, and her hands go to her belly. She doesn't argue with him.

Gabriel enjoys breakfast with us and spends a little more time with Ocran before placing him in his playpen and bidding us farewell. Tami watches from the window as Gabriel grabs his duffel bag and leaves the village.

"It could be years before he comes back," she mutters, and I bury my face in her neck, nuzzling her claim mark.

"It doesn't matter, as long as he comes back," I tell her. Tami turns around and wraps her arms around my neck, smiling at me lovingly.

"I'm serious about helping out. I know I'm pregnant right now and can't do much, but I want to help," she insists. I sigh and nod. It's better in these situations to just give Tami whatever she wants.

The happier she is, the better our bond will be. I love how she completes me. Tami's going to be pregnant nonstop for the next couple of years. She pulls back and runs a hand over my chest.

"I was thinking, maybe we could slow down after this baby so I can contribute to Wintermoon." She says. I glare at her. I don't like the sound of this. Slow down? What is she talking about? I remain quiet, waiting for her to finish.

"I'm not saying no sex or anything. I'm suggesting birth control. Just for a little while." I laugh at that. My sweetheart doesn't understand.

"Baby, I'll support any decision you make about children. As long as I get to keep you and the little ones we have, I'm happy. But birth control does not work with supernaturals. You'll have to stay off my dick," I say, then pull back from her.

The look on Tami's face is priceless, like I just stole candy from a baby. Her lips curl into a pout, and she looks like she wants to melt into the floor.

"Don't worry, baby. There are other ways we can pleasure each other. There's always oral until you're ready for me again." I turn to clean the kitchen, and she immediately chases after me.

"Wait!" she yells, grabbing my arm.

I stop and turn to face her, giving her a smug smile that I know she wants to slap off my face. If there's anything Tami loves more, it's riding me. Taking that from her is an immediate deal-breaker.

"I was just thinking about it. I never said I wanted to go through with it." I laugh, then grab the plates and go to the sink.

"Tami, I'll do whatever you want. The only thing I won't allow is for you, Ocran, or the baby you're carrying to leave me. You have to stay with me, baby."

"I never said I wanted to leave you. I love you, Kane. I just feel like I'm not contributing enough." I set the dishes down, then grip her waist and lift her onto the counter.

"Tami, there haven't been shifter children in a thousand years. Witches can procreate, but a child born out of love in a millennium is rare. You are contributing. But I'll never deny you your dreams. If you want a break from making babies, I'll give you that. But birth control doesn't work with us. Fate wants us to procreate." I place a gentle kiss on her forehead, and she cups my face, pulling me into a passionate kiss.

"I don't want you to take your dick away from me," she whispers, a mischievous smile on her lips. I glance at Ocran playing in the pen, then wrap my arms around her, lifting her and carrying her into the pantry.

"You own me, baby. Where do you want it?" I ask, pressing her against the wall. I unzip my pants and pull out my shaft, stroking it a few times before sliding her panties to the side. I line up at her entrance and feel her warmth envelop me.

"I want you inside me," she breathes, and I push inside her. She moans, her nails digging into my shoulders as she takes me deep. I grip her hips and guide her up and down on my length.

I can feel her heat and tightness around me, her breath quickening with every thrust. She bites her lip, focused and ready for more.

"Just like that," I murmur, my voice low as I quicken my pace. Each thrust drives deeper, mixing our gasps with the muffled sounds of Ocran in the background.

"Don't stop," she urges, and I feel a surge of excitement.

I drive harder, her body responding instinctively, meeting my thrusts with a hungry rhythm. Sweat beads on my forehead as I savor the way she moves, the way she feels.

"More," she pleads, and I nod, my grip tightening on her hips as I push deeper still.

Heat builds between us, our desire thick in the air. I can sense the tension as our breaths intermingle, quickening with urgency.

"Can you feel it?" I ask, my voice rough. "We're close."

Her eyes flutter shut, a satisfied smile breaking onto her face. "Together," she gasps.

With one final thrust, the pressure bursts, pulling us both into an overwhelming wave of pleasure.

My release fills her, though it's unnecessary now since her womb is already filled with our new baby. The sensation of her walls pulsating around me is intense.

"I love you; I love you; I love you," she murmurs over and over. I will never tire of this woman. I bury my face in her neck, my teeth grazing against her claim mark, feeling the urge to bite her again.

Well-bonded mates often claim each other multiple times. That's what I want with Tami. I want her to leave scars from her love bites all over my neck. Ocran starts to get fussy, and Tami giggles, trying to let herself down to tend to him, but I keep her in my arms.

"Let him wait a bit. I'll clean you up first, then you can go to him." Tami sighs clearly satisfied.

I carry her out of the pantry, my dick still inside her as I take a quick peek at Ocran, relieved he's fine. He just wants his mommy. Then, I carry her upstairs to the bathroom to help her get cleaned up.

If someone had told me Fate had this forever planned out for me a year ago when I was living on the border, I wouldn't have believed it. I thought Fate had given up on me.

But I was wrong. My Goddess, Fate, placed me there at just the right time so that I could be with Tami. I'll spend the rest of my days making sure Fate's choices were not made in vain. I'll cherish this love, this happiness forever, with Tami.

The only woman who could tame my wild wolf.

The End.

ABOUT THE AUTHOR

Tessa Stone

Tessa Stone writes stories about possessive supernatural alpha heroes who will do anything for their love interests. She loves iced coffee, books with obsessive protagonists, and playing The Sims 4. Tessa is a graduate student at Southern New Hampshire University, working toward an MFA in English, Creative Writing/Fiction. She lives in Wayne, Michigan, with her two daughters, ages 9 and 5, and two pets.

Follow me on my socials:

Facebook, Instagram, TikTok: @authortessatone

My website:

http://tessastone.com

Want to chat with the author? Join my Facebook Group

https://www.facebook.com/groups/blackvoicesinparanormalromance

Join my mailing list for my to get first access to my new releases, bonus scenes, and arc sign ups!

https://author-tessa-stone.ck.page/af76f4b807

ALSO BY TESSA STONE

What's Next?

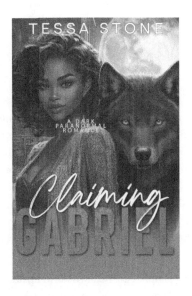

Claiming Gabriel

In a world of danger and destiny, Gabriel must rescue orphaned shifters while grappling with an irresistible bond to Olivia, the waitress who unwittingly becomes his fated mate.

Gabriel

I'm the last of my pack to find a mate, and it's agonizing. I crave the family life I've watched my brothers enjoy for years. So, I've chosen to assist Kade in rescuing baby shifters who are victims of an underground trafficking ring run by radical humans. It's a heartbreaking mission, saving orphaned shifter children, but it's necessary. I'm tired of seeing innocent supernaturals suffer at the hands of these extremists.

I suspected I might meet my fated mate on this journey, but I was still caught off guard by her sweet strawberry scent, one I'll never forget. Her name is Olivia, a young waitress from Downtown Detroit. She's unwittingly entangled with some radicals while trying to help two escaped shifter babies. She thinks she's doing a good deed by bringing the children to me, but how do I tell her she's destined to be mine forever?

Olivia

After finishing my night shift at the diner in Downtown Detroit, I never expected to find two little orphaned shifter children who had escaped an underground trafficking ring while I was taking out the trash in the back alley. I quickly brought them to my apartment for safety, but then I took them to the only place I knew could help—Thirst Trap, a nightclub in Downtown Detroit, run by supernaturals. That's where I met Gabriel, a stunning wolf shifter with the most captivating blue eyes I've ever seen.

What I thought would be a simple good deed—returning the children to their people—turned my world upside down. Gabriel claims I'm his fated mate, the woman chosen for him by the Goddess Fate. He's determined to keep me. I find myself traveling to Wintermoon, where I'm supposedly meant to spend the rest of my days with this enigmatic shifter. But I'm not ready to give in. He took me against my will, and the harder I try to resist him, the stronger this inexplicable connection grows. How can I escape this mysterious creature when he has already captured my body—and soon, my heart?

Made in the USA
Las Vegas, NV
10 November 2024

11461543R00121